The Blizzard Brides, Book 17

by Cat Cahill

Copyright

All rights reserved. No part of this publication may be reproduced, distributed, or transmitted in any form or by any means, including photocopying, recording, or other electronic or mechanical methods, without the prior written permission of the author, except in the case of brief quotations embodied in critical reviews and certain other noncommercial uses permitted by copyright law. For permission requests, write to the author at:
http://www.catcahill.com[1]

This is a work of fiction. Names, characters, businesses, places, events, locales, and incidents are either the products of the author's imagination or used in a fictitious manner. Any resemblance to actual persons, living or dead, or actual events is purely coincidental.

Copyright © 2021 Cat Cahill

Cover design by EDH Graphics

All rights reserved.

---

1. http://www.catcahill.com/

The Blizzard Brides

Welcome to Last Chance, Nebraska!

When the freak blizzard of 1878 kills most of the men in a small Nebraska town, what does it mean for the surviving women and children?

Realizing they need to find men of honor to help rebuild, the women place an advertisement in *The Matrimonial Times*.

Choosing a husband is more difficult than they thought, when there is an overwhelming response to the ad.

Will these Blizzard Brides find a second chance at love in a town called Last Chance?

[Join the Blizzard Brides Reader's Community](https://www.facebook.com/groups/theblizzardbrides)[1]

---

1. https://www.facebook.com/groups/theblizzardbrides

Chapter One

Last Chance, Nebraska — June 1879

She ought to take in a cat. Or perhaps a dog, but a cat would be easier.

Faith Thornton rested a hand on the envelopes that spilled across the post office counter, trying to imagine a cat curled up on the hearth across the room. Simply having another living being here with her all the time would be comforting.

She shook her head to clear the reverie and looked down at the work to be done. Since her husband Aaron had perished in the second blizzard last fall, Faith had run Last Chance's post and telegraph office on her own. Her sister Celia had helped, until she married and returned to her farm outside of town. And occasionally some of the other widows would stop in and assist, more for the company than anything else, but Faith didn't mind—either the help or the company.

One thing she had learned since last September was that being a widow was quite lonesome.

Not that she had any wish whatsoever to remarry. It didn't matter how much that irksome Pastor Barnaby Collins pressed her to find a husband or return to Mississippi, Faith had no intention of doing either. This business was Aaron's pride and joy. They'd worked it together since they arrived here, and it was a necessity in a town on the Western Nebraska prairie. Each time she sorted the mail or took down a message from the telegraph, she felt almost as if he were here again, looking over her shoulder and ready to meet her with a smile or a kiss.

That old familiar ache squeezed Faith's heart. She closed her eyes a moment, letting the feeling come and then letting it fade. Missing him hadn't grown easier, but she had learned to live with the feeling. In those first few months, the emptiness was all-consuming, and there were times she didn't know how she would face the next day. She leaned heavily on Celia, and on her friends in town, to simply survive.

But each day, the work awaited.

The mail didn't stop, and telegrams still clicked through over the wires the railroad had strung along to the town where they eventually planned to build tracks. Every day, no matter how broken she felt inside, Faith sat diligently at the table where the telegraph machine was set up and sent and received telegrams about urgent family matters, wanted men, business opportunities, and anything else folks deemed important enough to pay to send quickly over the wires.

"Faith?" Josie Gresham closed the front door behind her.

Faith blinked, trying to pull herself from her thoughts. That happened often since Aaron had passed. She'd find herself reminiscing about the times they'd shared, or wondering how things might have turned out differently, or any number of things that pulled her away from the reality set out before her. "Come on in," she said to her friend as she glanced down at the letters still spread out before her.

"I heard the stage brought in several pieces of mail." Josie's brown eyes flicked to the letters on the counter.

Faith gave her a warm smile. "I'll check." She sorted through the pile, her practiced eyes searching for Josie's name as her friend twisted the end of her ever-present long brown braid. "No letters here for you. Were you expecting one?"

Josie looked so slight inside the bulky men's shirt she wore, particularly as she leaned against the counter. "George thought I ought to write to one of the fellows who answered that advertisement last winter. He looked so twitchy that I thought he might have taken a page from my father's book and written on my behalf."

"Instead of being so concerned about you, your brother ought to do his part and marry one of the ladies who was widowed. At least we all know him, unlike these letter-writers." Faith pressed her fingers into the counter, her own little secret weighing on her mind.

Josie nodded. "That is precisely what I told him! Why is it that Pastor Collins feels he can harass us ladies, and yet leave men like George alone to do as they please? It isn't right."

Faith agreed wholeheartedly. She and Josie had entirely different reasons for not wanting to marry again, yet Pastor Collins didn't give one whit for their reasons. And, apparently, neither did George. As far as Faith was concerned, Josie's brother should count his lucky stars he'd been too sick to join the hunt or the search party that had perished in the blizzards last fall. His illness made him one of the few men left in the area, and yet no one pressured him to marry one of the many widows.

"Will you stay for tea?" Faith asked. "I was going to put some on as soon as I get these envelopes sorted."

"I can't today. I rode in for an order at the mercantile and, well..." She looked at the mess on the counter with a skeptical eye. "Anyhow, I need to get back to help George. Unless you'd prefer I stay?"

Faith's heart squeezed. Josie was like a little sister to her. They were as different as could be—Faith being ever the lady and Josie as wild as one of the bulls on the ranch where she was raised—but Josie had taken to Faith soon after she'd arrived in town with Aaron and Celia and Celia's late husband Ned. Despite her tendency for men's clothing and her penchant for speaking first and thinking later, Josie had quickly endeared herself to Faith, and Faith greatly looked forward to Josie's rides into town.

"I'm fine," Faith said truthfully. Only a few months ago, that would have been a lie, but with the onset of spring and the relief that came with having the missing men's bodies found and a proper memorial service held, some of the grief had given away to short little bursts of feeling almost normal. And the funny thing was, Faith rarely realized she'd reached one of those moments until something triggered the sadness again.

"I'm glad," Josie said with the sweet smile she gave genuinely to anyone who deserved it. "I should be back in town in a couple of days. I'll make time to visit a while then."

Faith bid goodbye to her friend and turned her attention to the envelopes again. In searching for Josie's name, she'd found herself also looking for her own name on the envelopes. But none had been addressed to Faith.

She pulled out two envelopes that had been forwarded from the matrimonial newspaper in New York. It had been several months since the widows in town had placed their advertisement for grooms, and yet letters still straggled in. All for the best though, considering some of the ladies were still looking for husbands.

But not Faith.

No man could ever replace Aaron, not in her life and certainly not in her heart. Although Pastor Collins was becoming more and more insistent that Faith choose a husband, she stood steadfast in her absolute refusal.

She set aside the sorted mail, propped open the door that led from the office to the rest of her home, and walked the short hallway to the kitchen. The building was a mere three rooms—a kitchen, a bedroom, and the front room, which served as both the parlor and the post and telegraph office. In the kitchen, she lit the stove and set the pot of water leftover from breakfast to heat for tea.

As she sat at the table to wait, a piece of paper rustled in the pocket of her skirt. Her heart thumping at the sound, Faith retrieved the letter and spread it out on the table before her. She read it again, her eyes traveling over the familiar words and a smile lifting her lips.

Mr. Beau Landry wrote the most entertaining letters. Never once had he failed to make her laugh, which was a feat rarely accomplished since Aaron had died. Faith didn't know what had possessed her to open that first letter on a cold February afternoon. Perhaps it was the address in New Orleans, so close to her childhood home in Mississippi, or maybe it was the fine handwriting on the envelope. She figured she would carefully slice open the letter forwarded from the New York newspaper, read it, and then simply reseal it and drop it into the stack of the other letters from potential grooms, which would be dispersed among the remaining widows in town.

But she hadn't put it back. Instead, his letter had brought a spark of joy to her broken heart, and she felt compelled to write to him. She'd sent the letter off to New Orleans with a nagging guilt. After all, Mr. Landry had written in search of a wife, and she certainly didn't want a husband.

She kept her missives short at first, just enough to convince him to write her in return. But her letters had grown steadily longer, and she'd found herself telling him things she'd not even shared with Celia or Josie. While her friends in town heard her reminiscences about Aaron and her great remorse at never having children with him, Mr. Landry heard about her childhood memories, funny instances around town, and dreams she'd buried with Aaron.

His letters—and hers to him—were an escape. And whether it was right or not, Faith thoroughly enjoyed them. Mr. Landry hadn't broached the subject of marriage at all, and because of that, Faith continued the correspondence.

And she would continue, so long as he didn't mention marriage.

And so long as he didn't simply show up in town the way Celia's now-husband, Jack Wendler, did, expecting to be married.

Chapter Two

Beauregard Landry tugged on the silk vest as he stepped down the hotel stairs. This suit had never fit well, and he wasn't certain what had gone through his mind when he'd chosen it from among others to bring here to Nebraska.

Leaving New Orleans as fast as possible, that was what had gone through his mind.

But that was all in the past. Here, in this town on the lonesome Nebraska plains, was his future. Sure, it had far fewer people than he ever could have imagined. And certainly, he'd counted only one theater. And of course, he appeared far overdressed compared to most of the men he'd seen. Yet none of that diminished his hope.

Because here in Last Chance, his wife-to-be awaited him.

Beau stepped out from the hotel door onto First Street. He could see the post and telegraph office off to the right, past the end of First Street and across Main Street. He took one step in that direction and froze.

What if she took one look at him and turned him away?

He'd spotted her yesterday, from a short distance, after he'd disembarked from the stagecoach. She'd stood outside her business—and what he presumed was also her home—speaking with another woman. He'd gaped at her like a man out of his mind.

Mrs. Faith Thornton was stunningly beautiful.

Beau didn't know what he'd expected. After all, they hadn't so much as described their appearances, never mind sent each other photographs. All he'd gathered from her letters was that she was approximately his age. She talked often of her work at the post and telegraph office, and so he'd surmised that one of the two ladies standing outside of it yesterday had to be her. When the other woman left, the lady who remained had to be Faith. Even from a distance, he'd been taken with her luminous skin, her light brown hair with golden strands lit from the sun, and her warm smile.

He could hardly contain himself then. He wanted to immediately introduce himself, but when the driver pointed out the nearest hotel and boarding house, Beau looked down at his dusty, wrinkled travel clothing, and realized he'd make a much better impression after a bath, a meal, and a good night of sleep.

Yet now that everything was all in order, he hesitated. It was an odd feeling. Beau hadn't paused before doing anything in his life. He attacked every moment with certainty and conviction. Sometimes it worked, such as the idea to sell his late father's newspaper business for a pretty penny, and other times . . . well. Those times were best not dwelled upon, particularly the one that caused his abrupt departure from Louisiana.

He glanced about at the ramshackle buildings that surrounded him and decided a walk about town was in order. He took off to the left, away from Main Street and the woman who awaited him, making his way past small homes and businesses.

Beau marveled at how quickly he reached the end of the road. Beyond the few homes that lined the cross street, tall, waving prairie grasses stretched far past what he could see. Off in the distance, imposing bluffs reminded him he was no longer in New Orleans.

He turned right. It was quiet this side of town, with fewer buildings and fewer people. How remarkable it was that two places could be so entirely different. New Orleans was busy, loud with people and the jangle of music, full of energy and a languid heat that permeated every breath one took. Last Chance felt like the country's last defense against the encroaching wilderness. And while it was warm—almost hot, even—the air felt lighter.

The walk cleared his mind and entertained him simultaneously. He nodded to various citizens, a couple here, an older lady there, a group of young women, and a couple of men who had a shady look about them.

He passed a cemetery adorned with small wooden crosses. A couple of ladies stood gathered there, clutching each other's arms and talking quietly. A fellow outside the nearby church that Beau presumed might be the minister leveled him with a gaze that made Beau walk faster. He had the distinct feeling the man wanted to reel him into a conversation, and while normally, Beau was inclined to talk with anyone from any walk of life, something about that minister made him feel as if he ought to move along.

He turned, eying the homes and businesses that stretched down the few blocks that made up Main Street. And there, near the end and just before the depot, stood the Last Chance Post and Telegraph Office.

A GROOM FOR FAITH

Beau straightened, pulled again on his vest, and ventured forward. He had nothing to gain by avoiding the place, and everything to win by finally introducing himself to Faith.

Should he call her Faith? That was how she'd begun signing her letters to him. But considering they hadn't been introduced in person, perhaps he should address her as Mrs. Thornton? Or would she consider that a slight somehow?

He ought to have run that question by his mother before he left, but there hadn't been time even to tell her goodbye. What he'd give right now to have her advice. She'd encouraged his letters to Faith, and he secretly thought she hoped to get him out of New Orleans, where he'd fallen far too easily into the habit of stirring up trouble since he'd sold his father's business.

Beau squared his shoulders as he approached the post and telegraph office. He hoped she would be happy to see him. They'd never discussed the subject of matrimony in their letters, but that *was* the reason Faith and the other ladies in town had placed their advertisement. Surely she expected him to offer to marry her. Why else would she have continued writing him?

Although she likely presumed he would announce his intention to travel to Last Chance, rather than simply show up one day.

He opened the door carefully, uncertain what to expect on the other side. The room was empty. No one stood on either side of the counter that spanned the width of the long room to the left. A conversational setting of chairs and a settee sat about a cold fireplace to the right. Another door stood closed straight ahead. Beau supposed that led back to the building's living quarters, where Faith likely was at that moment.

What should he do now? Knock on that door? Wait patiently for her return? Leave and come back another time? He tugged on that blasted vest again. His first order of business after meeting Faith would be to find a clothier or tailor. It was ridiculous to keep something so uncomfortable when he could easily afford to replace it.

Perhaps he'd do that now, and then come back another day—ideally with a better-fitting suit. He had just turned when the door opened.

"Oh, hello," a friendly feminine voice said. "I'm sorry, I didn't realize you were here. Do you need to post a letter or send a telegram?"

Beau turned around, and there she was, even more perfect up close. He blinked at her, unable to believe what he saw before him. She narrowed green eyes that reminded him of the leaves on a live oak as he stood there speechless. Then she tilted her head just so, as if she were trying to figure him out. Faith was several inches shorter than he was, and pretty blue earbobs danced when she straightened her head again. The jewelry matched the sky blue skirt she wore with a plain white shirtwaist. But what she wore hardly mattered. This woman would be stunning in a rice sack.

Her smile turned cautious. "Did you need help?"

He swept off his hat, far too late to be gentlemanly. "I apologize. I didn't mean to disrupt your work."

"It's no disruption." She swept up her skirts in her hand and moved like a boat on still water across the room and behind the counter. "Now, what do you need? To post a letter?"

Beau swallowed, unfamiliar nerves making him feel uncertain of himself—which was not something he'd ever felt before. "I have no letter or telegram to send."

She tilted her head again, those emerald eyes still on him. "Are you waiting on a letter, then? There's been no mail since yesterday, and—"

He shook his head.

A cross between amusement and the beginnings of impatience lifted her lips and tightened them at the same time. "Might I ask why you're here, then?"

"Well, Mrs. . . . Faith. I'm Beau Landry."

Chapter Three

Once, when Faith was young, she and Celia and some of the other girls who lived near their family farm, had run races up and down the dirt road for hours in the dead of August with no water. She'd thought she'd been thirsty then.

But that was no match for how dry Faith's throat went now.

"I'm sorry. You're . . ." That was all she could manage to say.

"Beau Landry." The devilishly handsome man spun his fine hat in his hands before continuing in a lightly accented voice. "Your . . . correspondent, I suppose?"

"Correspondent," Faith repeated, simply because she didn't know what else to say. And she was not one to ever find herself at a loss for words. She gripped the edge of the counter.

He was here.

How was he here?

Why was he here?

Her memory charged through every letter she'd received from him, searching for mention of his actually coming to Last Chance, but the memories were jumbled and hazy and she couldn't force her mind to slow and think properly.

His brow creased now, and he transferred the hat to his left hand and reached out to her with his right. "Would you care to sit? You look faint, *cher*."

She dropped her incredulous eyes from his face to his broad shoulders to the assured outstretched hand. "I am not faint." And what was it he'd called her?

His mouth twitched as if she perplexed him somehow. Another moment went by and he withdrew his hand, but he kept those golden brown eyes on her as if he were trying to figure her out.

It was too much. Too unexpected.

The walls of the building were suddenly much too close, and Faith could not draw a deep breath. She had to get out.

Pushing herself away from the counter, she mumbled her excuses to this man who claimed to be Beau Landry, and propelled herself from behind the counter.

And then straight out the door.

*****

Outside, Faith drew in deep breaths of the warm summer air as she strode headlong down the road. Past the stagecoach depot next door, she made an abrupt turn onto the road that led down to the river and the ferry. Someone called to her. Whether it was the ferryman, a friend, or that dark-haired man who'd just turned her entire world upside down, Faith didn't know. She didn't answer and she didn't look back.

Simply breathing and placing one foot in front of the other were all she could handle right now.

She turned around the back of the depot and pressed ahead along the River Road. She drew up near a group of cottonwoods by the river, grabbing onto the trunk to steady herself as her breath came quickly.

Faith stared out at the muddy North Platte as it meandered past Last Chance and tried to untangle her thoughts.

He was *here*.

She squeezed her eyes shut. She shouldn't have written him. That awful guilt she felt each time she added her letter to the bag she passed onto the stage driver came rolling over her in waves now. It had been cruel to let him believe she was interested in . . . what, exactly? Matrimony?

Faith's stomach flipped at the very thought. She pried her eyes open again and tried to focus on the gentle flow of the river. She hadn't agreed to any such thing. Why, neither she nor Beau had even mentioned it in their correspondence.

So why had he come?

"Faith?" That languid, smooth voice interrupted her thoughts, and when she turned, he was there. Standing just a few feet away was the man she never expected nor intended to meet in person.

"I'm sorry, should I call you Mrs. Thornton? I don't know the conventions for a situation such as this." He chuckled lightly, and Faith's stomach flipped yet again.

She shook her head. She ought to insist he call her Mrs. Thornton, and yet it felt odd to think of him as Mr. Landry, not when she already knew the names of his parents, his sisters and their husbands, and even the name of the road where he'd grown up in New Orleans.

A GROOM FOR FAITH

He took a step closer, his fine shoes sinking in the soft ground. He must have left his hat behind in his haste to come after her, as it was nowhere to be seen now.

"I apologize for arriving unannounced," he said, his voice like velvet. How could a man have a voice so rich? And that accent made him sound as if he were from a foreign country, somewhere exotic and far, far away from Nebraska.

When she said nothing, he pressed on. "I thought it might be a nice surprise, given how long we've corresponded." He paused. "I must confess, I didn't expect to find you so beautiful."

A short laugh escaped Faith's throat. "You decided on a whim to travel hundreds of miles to meet a woman you imagined might resemble an ogre?"

She'd caught him off guard, that much was evident in the way his eyes widened and his mouth opened. Something about that pleased Faith mightily.

"No! No, of course not. It's only that I didn't expect, well . . ." He trailed off, and Faith allowed herself a slight grin as she looked toward the river.

But she didn't stop him for long. Taking another step around her, he said, "I thought I might stay at the hotel and we could get to know one another better. That's far easier done in person than in letters, don't you think? I can treat you to dinners and walks along the river. I believe I saw a theater—"

"What makes you think I enjoy such amusements?"

His forehead wrinkled. She could tell she was shattering all of his preconceived notions he'd likely dreamed up on the train north, and she was glad.

Mostly.

She shook that last thought away and kept her eyes locked with his, waiting for an answer.

"Well, I mean, of course you must enjoy something. One cannot work all the time. You name the activity, and I'd be happy to escort you." He gave her a smile that matched the slow, easy timbre of his voice, and Faith nearly shivered.

He was far too intriguing.

She needed to keep her guard up, else she turn into her sister and go all dreamy-eyed over a good-looking man with a talent for words. She knew better than that. Faith had dealt with her share of men who'd wandered into town upon hearing of the husband-searching widows, presumed she was one of them, and then tried to impress her and flirt with her. She was well-practiced at leveling them with a cold stare and clipped words.

She ought to do the same with Beau.

And yet instead she found herself saying, "I enjoy meeting up with the other ladies to sew together. And sometimes I look forward to helping at the livery."

The latter wasn't true, but it was worth it to see this man taken aback. He blinked at her, and Faith chewed a corner of her lip to keep from laughing.

"Well . . . I'm happy to escort you to any of those occasions. I can't say I'm much for sewing, but I have objections to horses." He pulled at the hem of his vest as if it weren't particularly comfortable.

"Hmm," was all she said. The man had a sunny disposition that matched his eyes. Faith was almost certain that if she told him that a plague of locusts was scheduled to arrive tomorrow, he'd smile and ask if she'd like to stroll along the river before they arrived.

"Why don't we have supper together tonight?" he said. "I've taken a room at the hotel. We could eat there or—"

"I've beans soaking already."

"I like beans."

Faith exhaled, turning toward the river. The man was infuriating. Couldn't he see she had no interest whatsoever in courting?

"Faith," he said in a more serious voice.

She glanced back at him, at those eyes that were a startling shade of amber she didn't think she'd ever seen before. He ran a hand through his thick, dark hair, and he looked as if he were trying to find the right words to say.

"Yes?" she prompted. She needed to return home. For all she knew, an urgent message was coming over the wire right now, and no one was there to take it down.

"Why did you write to me?"

Faith swallowed. That was the question she'd asked herself each time she posted a letter to him.

He watched her, waiting for an answer, and when she didn't give one, that smile slowly returned to his face. "We needn't marry immediately, of course. I'll pay you another visit tomorrow."

Marry? Pay her another visit? Faith pinched her lips together to keep from sputtering some half thought out response. She forced herself to breathe normally, kept her eyes on his, and then finally said, as coolly as possible, "I must return to my work."

She brushed past him and climbed up the slight embankment back toward River Road.

Behind her, Beau Landry laughed in such a way that reminded her of melted chocolate. "Until tomorrow!"

Faith huffed and walked faster. She had no need of a suitor, and certainly no need for a husband.

Chapter Four

The next morning, Beau whistled as he left Dawson's Diner. This little town was beginning to grow on him. The people were friendly enough, and the breakfast he'd just put away ensured he wouldn't be hungry again until dark. He thought he might finally pay a visit to the tailor to order a better-fitting suit. And then . . . He smiled at the post and telegraph office across the street.

Then he'd pay another visit to Faith.

If he'd been taken with her words in the letters she'd written, that was nothing compared to how much space she'd occupied in his mind since he finally met her. She'd been clear in her letters that her husband's death had been hard on her. Perhaps that was why she was so reticent to get to know him better.

And yet she'd written to him. Letter after letter after letter. Something about him interested her. And Beau was determined to wait as long as it took before she remembered that.

He stepped away from the diner, thinking vaguely that the tailor was in the direction of the church, toward the west. It was a beautiful day, with fluffy white clouds sliding slowly across a bright blue sky. It was already warm, which meant it was likely to grow hot by the height of the day. Yet hot here was nothing compared to the heat of New Orleans. The heat here warmed your bones instead of melting them.

He strode along the town's Main Street, giving friendly nods and greetings to those he passed and wondering what it might be like to settle here. He'd run the post and telegraph office, of course. Faith could teach him all he needed to know. They'd operate the business together, he'd hold a place of standing in this town, have a purpose. That purpose was what he lacked back at home, he knew now.

He'd never been cut out to be a newspaperman, and selling that business was in his—and his mother's—best interest. But the problem he hadn't yet discerned at that point was what he'd do with himself afterward. Without acting as his father's assistant, he had no real purpose in his life.

And so he'd fallen into the wrong sorts of amusements.

Beau shuddered as that night that had changed everything ran through his mind again. That was what had finally woken him up from the drifting life he'd led. He'd made a terrible, necessary decision that night. And that decision had driven him right out of Louisiana and into this new life.

And he was determined to make the best of it, starting with Faith.

As he grew closer to the end of Main Street, the church and the nearby tailor's storefront came into sight—along with a sight Beau surely would never grow tired of.

Faith.

She stood in front of the park across the road from the undertaker and the tailor, and she was speaking with . . . Beau squinted as he attempted to make out the man's face. It was

A GROOM FOR FAITH

the preacher, he thought. The same one who'd eyed him with undisguised curiosity yesterday. Well, he ought to make the man's acquaintance, given that he was planning to live here.

Beau crossed the road, a friendly smile already in place, until he grew close enough to hear what the man was saying to Faith.

". . . I worry about all of my flock, including you, Mrs. Thornton."

"I assure you, Pastor, I'm doing just fine. I have thoughtful friends to provide me with company and help when I need it with my work. You needn't worry about me." Faith's words were polite, but her voice held a slight edge. Beau immediately had the feeling that she'd had this conversation with the preacher before.

The pastor folded his hands together in front of him, almost as if he were about to begin praying right there on the dirt road in front of the park. "That isn't enough, my dear. You need a husband. This is no place—"

"For a lady alone. Yes, Pastor, I remember." Faith dug a hand into her skirts, and her voice went from the edge of polite to testy. "However—"

"My dear, if you cannot find a husband, I'm afraid I'll have no choice but to contact the railroad and request they send us a man to take over the telegraph and the mail."

Faith's face paled. Beau forced himself to remain where he was, despite every urge he had to stride forward and tell that preacher exactly what he thought of the man's plan to take Faith's livelihood out from beneath her.

"Pastor, my work—*Aaron's* work—means everything to me," Faith said softly, a proud ship with her sails deflated.

"And you need a man to run it properly."

Beau swallowed a chuckle. He doubted there was a man alive more competent than Faith in running that office. Apparently Faith agreed, as she drew herself up taller and balled her fists at her sides as the color returned to her face. A wagon clattered behind Beau, drawing her attention momentarily away from the minister.

Her eyes alighted on Beau. He gave her an encouraging smile, ready to see her tell that man exactly how well she'd done her job. But instead of turning back to the preacher, she held a hand out to Beau.

"Well, you'll be pleased, Pastor Collins," she said. "Because Mr. Landry has just recently arrived in town. We've been corresponding for some time."

Beau hesitated for only a fraction of a second before moving forward to take her gloved hand into his own. He inclined his head toward the pastor. "Beauregard Landry," he said. "From New Orleans. It's a pleasure to meet you."

It took every ounce of self-restraint he had not to laugh at Pastor Collins' pinched face. It was as if the man truly would have taken joy from removing Faith from her post and sending her away on the next stage, back to Mississippi. As if all she'd done for this town meant nothing at all.

"Barnaby Collins, pastor," the man said almost primly.

"Well, isn't that a fine coincidence, *cher*?" Beau said to Faith.

She furrowed her brow as her fingers tensed under his. He had the distinct feeling she wanted to slap him. "What do you mean?"

"To run into the pastor like this when we were just speaking of—"

"Marriage! Yes, yes. I'd be pleased to marry you today, of course." Pastor Collins looked at them expectantly.

It was precisely what Beau was hoping the man would say, but Faith stared at the minister with her mouth slightly agape before turning to stare daggers at Beau.

"That would be perfect. Shall we say five o'clock?" Beau asked, tightening his hand around Faith's in a gesture he hoped was reassuring.

Pastor Collins agreed to the time, offered them both his congratulations, and scurried off to annoy who knew what other lady in town.

The moment the man was out of sight, Faith wrenched her hand from Beau's. "How dare you! I have no interest whatsoever in marrying you. You might go to the church at five o'clock, but I assure you, Mr. Landry, I will *not* be there."

Chapter Five

Faith felt as if she were made of fire. Flames licked her words and her thoughts, and she wanted nothing more than to throw them all at the man who'd put her into this position.

Beau removed his hat, as if he were penitent. "Please, Faith, hear me out."

Listening was the last thing she wanted to do. In fact, she doubted she was capable of anything at that moment aside from screaming to the heavens. She ground her fingertips into her palms and fixed him with a glare. "Why should I? How dare you presume so much? How dare you decide to insert yourself into my life!"

"Don't you see it was your only option?" he said quietly.

She stood there, her chest heaving with more unsaid words. "You are *not* my only option."

"No, I'm not. You've likely had your choice of men, yet you chose to write to me. And now I'm here, and like it or not, I'm going to help you save your business and remain in this town. Unless you'd prefer to return to your parents in Mississippi?"

A GROOM FOR FAITH

Faith blinked at him, momentarily stunned by the forcefulness of his words. She drew in a breath, ready to retort, when he wrapped a hand around each of her arms. She froze.

"Faith," he said gently. "I'm offering you the perfect solution. Not only will you get to continue the work you love so much, you'll have me to help you with it. How many nights have you sat up late, waiting for an urgent telegram?"

She pressed her lips together. More nights than she could count, but she didn't want to give him the satisfaction of knowing he was right. Besides, it was a little hard to think with the warmth of his hands wrapped about her arms.

"How many times have you wished you could join a friend for tea or simply take a stroll without having to hunt down someone to cover your station and hope he writes down any message that arrives correctly?"

Faith bit her lip. She hadn't taught anyone the code—she simply hadn't the time. Instead, friends who sat in for her simply wrote down how many short and long clicks came through over the telegraph, and then Faith had to sit down and make sense of their notes. To have someone who actually understood the message as it came through . . .

Except it meant she had to marry.

And she had to marry a man who was not Aaron.

"You don't understand," she said, trying in vain to keep the anguish from her voice. "I can't. Aaron—" She couldn't finish, not without risking tears. She pulled against his grip, needing the space to keep herself from completely falling apart.

Beau dropped his hands, and his face softened and looked, she thought, a little sad. "A marriage will keep the pastor out of your business. You'll keep your work, which I know means so much to you. And you'll have a partner to help you with it."

Faith swallowed before looking up at him. Kind amber eyes looked back at her. It was such a mesmerizing color—one that was hard to look away from. Why was he being so kind to her? It made no sense, given the way she'd treated him since his arrival. "I don't understand. What do you get from this arrangement?"

He frowned for a moment, looking off in the distance over her shoulder, before composing himself and replacing that frown with a smile. "I get to marry a beautiful woman."

Now it was Faith's turn to frown. "Flattery will get you nowhere. *If* I agree to this, it will be a marriage in name only."

"I'll accept those terms. Although I can't promise I won't try and change your mind."

"Hmph." Faith crossed her arms at his impertinence.

"Please," he said, more seriously. "Let me help you. It's why I came here."

Faith couldn't fathom what she might have said in any of her letters that indicated she needed rescuing. But he was here, and for reasons she couldn't comprehend, she trusted him. It would get Pastor Collins out of her business, and Beau could be a help . . .

"All right," she said, against her better judgment. "Five o'clock. It's barely enough time to alert my sister."

"I'll take care of that," Beau said. "You go back to work, and I'll ensure everything is ready."

Faith looked at him skeptically.

"Go on." He nodded toward the post and telegraph office.

She did need to get back. Young Nate Hallowell was watching the telegraph for her while she ran out to fetch some sundries—none of which she'd purchased given her untimely meeting with the pastor.

After another half moment of hesitation, she hurried back to work and let the day's activities occupy her mind rather than her upcoming nuptials. When Celia slipped through the door at four o'clock, she found Faith diligently sweeping the floor.

"Is it true?" her sister demanded, pressing her back to the door as she watched Faith.

"Unfortunately, yes." Faith couldn't meet Celia's eyes. It was far too embarrassing to admit she was doing exactly the thing she'd warned her sister against all those months ago—marrying a man she barely knew.

Although it had certainly worked out for Celia and Jack.

"Faith!" Celia ran to her and wrapped her arms around Faith's shoulders. Her growing stomach pressed against Faith. "I'm so happy for you! You must have a good feeling about him, then, right? Is he here? Why didn't you tell me you were writing to someone? How long have you been corresponding? Are you excited? Why aren't you dressed?"

Faith clung to her broom through the barrage of questions. To most people, Faith was the outgoing, friendly sister while Celia, who was only a few years older, was the more reserved of the two. But Celia had never been quiet around Faith, and Faith always thought her sister saved up all her words for those she felt most comfortable around.

"I am dressed," she finally said, pointedly ignoring the other questions. "How are you feeling?" Celia's pregnancy hadn't entirely agreed with her stomach.

Celia brushed off Faith's question with a wave of her hand. "I'm fine. But you can't wear an old work dress. Here—" Celia took the broom and laid it against the wall before dragging Faith back to her bedroom and throwing open her wardrobe. She presented Faith with a bodice and overskirt that went with a matching set of skirts in lovely shade of periwinkle. "This will be perfect. Put these on and I'll fix your hair."

"This is entirely unnecessary," Faith said, although she took the clothing from Celia. "I'm only marrying him to keep Pastor Collins from taking my work and giving it to some undeserving man from the railroad."

"Hmm." Celia looked at Faith a moment. "Do you know what you need? Fresh flowers for your hair. I'll go see if I can find some."

"Did you hear me?" Faith called after Celia as she left the room.

Celia turned back to her from where she stood at the door to the front room. "I heard you. Now get dressed."

Faith wanted to throw the clothing at Celia, but none of this was her sister's fault. Celia hadn't agreed to Beau's proposal.

Proposal. Faith could have laughed as she began to pull off her work dress in her bedroom. That would have indicated something romantic. Aaron had asked Faith to marry him by a lake back in Mississippi. He'd handed her a rose cut from his mother's garden, gotten down on one knee, and confessed he couldn't live the rest of his life without her.

The memory was so vivid that Faith drew in a sharp breath. They'd loved each other so much. She would never forget him.

And she certainly wouldn't replace him so easily with another man.

She peered at her reflection in the glass on her dressing table as she buttoned the bodice. She would marry Beau Landry.

But she would never fall in love with him.

Chapter Six

"Two long presses is the letter I, right?" Beau said, pencil in his hand.

"No, it's M. Letter I is two short presses." Faith imitated the clicks and clacks the telegraph machine would make for each type of press.

"Right." Beau looked at the jumble of letters he'd attempted to translate from Faith's pretend Morse code. "How long did it take you to remember all of this?"

Faith shrugged. "A few days, I think. I can't remember. Aaron and I learned it together."

"Hmm." It had been only a day. But he hadn't expected it to be such a challenge to remember.

The machine clicked, and he nearly jumped out of his chair. Faith smothered a laugh. "It's an incoming telegram. I'll take it down, but you should try too."

He nodded and listened intently as a series of clicks came intermittently. Beau wrote down his best guess and handed it to Faith when it finished.

"STNG DLAXED BHYENN," she read from his piece of scrap paper. "Well. That's close."

Beau frowned. "It makes no sense whatsoever. What is the actual message?"

Faith grinned and handed him the paper upon which she'd translated the telegram.

"Stage delayed, Cheyenne." He looked up. "Well, I suppose that's a more sensible sort of thing to send over a telegraph wire."

Faith burst into laughter at that, and Beau crumpled his paper. "How about I refill the inkwells instead?"

"I promise you'll catch on. It's like learning another language. Would you like to inform the depot that the stage from Cheyenne is delayed instead?"

Beau nodded gratefully and took the message from Faith. The depot was immediately next door, so the trip took but a few minutes. When he returned, Faith had busied herself with refilling the inkwells she kept on hand for customers needing to pen a letter or write out a telegram.

He watched her a moment, marveling at how much she had done on her own. In the months since her husband had died, she'd kept this place going—not an easy feat for one person.

And now he was her husband.

Beau grinned at the thought. She'd been quiet through the ceremony the day before, so much so that he'd worried something was wrong with her. Faith's sister, Mrs. Wendler, and her husband Jack had treated them to an evening meal purchased at the diner, and Faith had seemed more at ease while they ate. As soon as they returned home, he offered to make himself up a bed on the settee in the parlor area of the office. She fetched him linens and then made excuses to turn in early. And so Beau had spent his wedding night sitting in front of a fire he'd started more for the company than for the warmth and wondering if he'd done the right thing.

But when morning came, Faith seemed much more cheerful. She'd even made him eggs and fried up bacon as she discussed the intricacies of being the town's postmaster and telegraph operator. He'd kept up the conversation, happy to see her more comfortable with him, but wondering if her hesitation and pensiveness still lurked underneath the cheer.

She'd gone on to be friendly and lighthearted in conversation all day, and he'd begun to wonder if perhaps he'd imagined her reticence the evening before. He suspected she hadn't fully grieved the loss of her first husband, even though she hadn't said as much. Everyone he'd met in town had nothing but good things to say about the late Mr. Thornton, and Beau realized quickly he had big shoes to fill.

So long as Faith realized he wasn't trying to take the man's place. He'd learned that the hard way after his father had passed. No one could replace the elder Mr. Landry, least of all his less business-minded son. Beau had tried mightily for a year, and then finally confessed to his mother that he wasn't cut out to run a newspaper. To his everlasting surprise, Maman had simply taken his hand and told him that was all well and good and why had he waited so long to come to this understanding?

Having made that mistake once, he wouldn't do it again. He was no Aaron Thornton, he wouldn't pretend to be, and he hoped Faith understood that.

"Why are you staring at me so?" she asked, not looking up from the jar she filled with ink. "It's disconcerting."

"Perhaps I was simply admiring my wife."

She looked up at him sharply. "You can stop flirting with me. We're already married."

"Which was apparently not your intention in writing to me. I am curious, Mrs. Landry. Why did you respond to my letter, then, if not for purposes of marriage?" Beau sat in one of the chairs and eyed her, waiting for a response to the question that had plagued him the most since meeting her.

She set the ink bottle down but made no move to join him near the fireplace. "I was lonely, and I found your letter entertaining. That was all. *I* find it curious that you traveled all the way here for someone to whom you'd never once mentioned marriage. Why is that, Mr. Landry?" she countered.

Beau sucked in a cheek, trying not to laugh at her ability to immediately turn the table. She was no wilting flower, this woman he'd talked into marrying him. But what should he tell her? The real reason was harrowing and not something that was fit for feminine ears, much less anything he wanted to remember. Coming here, he'd hoped never to have to think about it again.

He opted for part of the story, one that excluded the worst parts. "My father founded the largest newspaper in the parish, which I believe I mentioned in one of my letters. I tried to run it after his death, but I fear I'm not much of a businessman, nor do I have much interest in newspapers. So I sold the business, with my mother's blessing. After that, I had no real direction in my life. I didn't know what I wanted to do, and finding myself quite taken with the letters I'd been receiving from a beautiful woman in west Nebraska, I decided that I might like to be married and to set up some sort of opportunity for myself in the town of Last Chance."

Faith came around from behind the counter and stood behind the chair across from Beau. "I believe you're telling me the truth, but I'm not a fool. I also believe there is far more to your truth than you're letting on."

He blinked at her. The woman was incredibly insightful. Too insightful. Not wanting to frighten her with the remainder of his story, he jumped up. "Let's get back to work. I'm determined to have this code memorized by nightfall."

He could feel her eyes on his back as he crossed behind the counter again. And he told himself he was doing the right thing by not saying more. She deserved a good man, one who would care for her and ensure that she kept this business she loved so much. The man he was now.

She certainly didn't deserve a reformed gambler who had blood on his hands—the man he was in New Orleans.

Chapter Seven

True to his word, Beau had memorized the Morse code for the telegraph in one day. The man was certainly determined, if nothing else. Another message had come in that evening, and he'd transcribed it perfectly.

And when Celia arrived in town late the next morning, Beau urged Faith to enjoy tea with her sister in the kitchen while he manned the office. Reluctant to leave everything in his hands, Faith finally acquiesced after he assured her he would retrieve her immediately if there was an emergency.

Now, as she sipped a soothing chamomile tea with Celia, Faith found her mind wandering back to the man at the front of the building. Why was he so assured and so determined to do right by her? He barely knew her.

"How are you finding married life again?" Celia asked with a slight grin. Her sister might be the quieter of the two, but Faith knew better. Celia's red hair had come with a streak of mischievousness that not many people saw.

"Oh, hush. He might hear you!"

Celia made a face over her tea. "He couldn't possibly. And you didn't answer my question."

"We're hardly married," Faith said. She set her teacup down and frowned at it. "And you know how I felt about Aaron."

Celia reached across the table and laid a hand on Faith's arm. "I do. But I also fully believe that Aaron wouldn't want you to live the rest of your life alone."

Faith squeezed her eyes shut. She wouldn't cry. She'd already done enough of that for five widows in the past several months.

"Mr. Landry seems quite taken with you. And I think he was awfully gallant to swoop in and save you from Pastor Collins."

"I know." Faith stared at her tea. "I don't understand why. I haven't been particularly kind to him since he arrived here. I ran out on him, in fact. All the way to the river. He followed me." She glanced up at Celia.

Her sister's lips lifted in a smile. "I'm not surprised."

"But *why*? Why does he care so much?" The thought kept Faith up at night. She'd done nothing at all to deserve such kind treatment from a man who hardly knew her.

"How many letters did you exchange with him?" Celia asked.

Faith shrugged. "I'm not certain. Several."

"So many that you lost track of the number?"

"I suppose. What does that have to do with anything? I only met him three days ago."

Celia cradled her teacup in her hands. "I'll tell you what I think. I believe that man fell in love with you from your letters."

Faith gave a short laugh. "That's impossible."

"Is it? Or do you say that only because it's never happened to you?"

Faith chewed on her lip. Was it possible? She couldn't think of what she could have written to Beau to engender such affection. "He didn't even know what I looked like."

"Does that matter so much? Would you have loved Aaron any less if his eyes were a different color, or heaven forbid, he'd lost an arm or a leg?" Celia sipped her tea as Faith considered the question.

"Not at all. But—"

"But nothing. It's the person you fall in love with, and you, Faith, are quite an incredible person."

"You're only saying that because you're my sister."

"Nonsense. Everyone in town would agree with me." Celia took another sip of tea while Faith's grew cold. "You ought to give him a chance."

"I can't do that." Faith toyed with the lace edging of the tablecloth she'd made back in Mississippi, soon after Aaron had proposed.

"Promise me you'll think about it," Celia said. "I don't think God would have sent Mr. Landry here if he didn't want you to be happy."

It wasn't that easy, though. Celia couldn't understand. Her marriage to Aaron's sterner, cold brother Ned had been miserable. When Ned perished in the blizzard, Celia was more than willing to take a second chance at a new life with someone else.

But if Faith opened her heart to Beau, where would that leave her love for Aaron? Even if Celia were right and Aaron would want her to find happiness again, that didn't make it feel like any less of a betrayal. What she'd had with Aaron had been perfect—all too short and all too wonderful. It felt wrong to set that aside for someone new.

No matter how much he made her laugh. Or how much he flattered her. Or that his smile made her feel as if her sorrows were a million miles away.

"I'll think about it," she said. "That's all I can promise."

When she saw Celia out, Beau politely opened the door for Faith's sister and offered to drive her back to her farm. Celia declined and raised her eyebrows at Faith. Faith could almost hear the words that came along with that look.

"I promise," she said, somewhat crossly.

"Good. I'll see you soon."

When Beau shut the door, Faith could feel his eyes on her as she crossed the room back to the counter.

"What did you promise?" he asked.

Faith's face went warm at the very thought of Beau discovering their conversation. "Nothing important."

"Hmm. Something so unimportant it makes you turn as red as a ripe apple." He leaned casually against the counter as Faith resorted an already sorted stack of envelopes. "That makes me even more curious, *cher*."

"It's nothing." Faith tapped the envelopes into a perfectly neat stack. "And what is that you're calling me?"

He gave her a slow smile, arms crossed lazily over his chest. "*Cher* . . . it's a term of endearment."

Faith's cheeks went warm and she stared down at the envelopes.

"Let's see . . ." he said when she didn't speak. "It can't be anything mundane. Was it a promise to bake a pie for your husband?"

Faith eyed him with a look she hoped said he'd be lucky to even get supper.

"No pie? All right . . . Maybe a promise to join your husband for a buggy ride along the river?"

"We can't leave the telegraph."

"We can if we get someone to watch it. Perhaps that boy Nate you have fill in sometimes." When she didn't reply, he continued. "Or maybe your promise was to listen to your husband's long-winded stories about his school days? They're quite entertaining, I assure you. I have one particularly good story involving a spider and an arithmetic lesson."

When Faith looked up from her envelopes again, he waggled his eyebrows, and she burst out into laughter. "You are incorrigible."

"I've been told that before."

"Tell me something," she said, her hands resting on the letters. "Why didn't you marry a nice girl in New Orleans? Surely you could have had your pick of possible wives."

"Is that a compliment? Are you flattering me, Mrs. Landry?"

Faith picked up one of the envelopes and swatted at him. "I'm serious. Why didn't you marry a girl and stay home? Why take a chance on me, clear out here?"

He watched her for a moment, and her heart sped up. Could Celia have been right? Had he fallen in love with her simply from her letters?

"I looked forward to your letters more than I looked forward to conversation with anyone else," he finally said.

Faith swallowed. Celia *was* right. It made no sense at all, but it was true. "I don't understand how."

His lips curved up into that lazy smile. It reminded her of long summer Sundays in Mississippi. "I don't either. But that's when I knew I wanted to marry you."

Faith's cheeks went warm again. None of this made any sense whatsoever, but she'd be lying if she said she didn't like the way he made her feel.

So long as she didn't think too hard about it, anyway.

He raised a hand and let his fingers drift slowly across her cheek. "You're even more beautiful when you blush."

It was too much—the words, the touch of his hand, the way his golden eyes seemed to melt her insides. Faith cleared her throat and took a step backward. "I thought I told you that flattery would get you nowhere."

He grinned and leaned an elbow on the counter. "I know. I like that about you too."

Faith wanted to throw her hands up. This man confused her more than anyone had in her entire life. Instead, she busied herself with dusting the already clean counter. "Why don't you make yourself useful and—"

The telegraph clicked at that moment, and Beau slid around the counter to take the seat before the machine, pencil and paper already in hand. Faith stood behind him, dust rag dangling from her hand, and eyes wide as he wrote down the message.

"It's a reply to the telegram Mrs. Purcell sent earlier," he said. "From her brother in St. Louis. If you'll be all right, I'll run this message over to her husband's office."

Faith nodded slowly, and before she knew it, Beau had grabbed his hat and was out the door.

Who was this man? Beau Landry was far more accomplished than she ever could have imagined.

And for some reason, he'd chosen her, the one woman who couldn't return his love.

Chapter Eight

Beau opened the door with a flourish. There, parked just out front of the post and telegraph office, was a shiny black buggy, recently cleaned and rented with a pair of fine horses from the livery.

Faith stood hesitantly in the doorway. "We can't. The telegraph—"

"I've already taken care of that. Young Mr. Hallowell here is eager to learn how to operate a telegraph. I offered to teach him if he could continue to man the machine and the office for us for an hour here and there." Beau extended an arm toward the young man who stood nearby, hat clasped in one hand and the buggy lines in the other.

"But— but he only just watched the telegraph the other day. I try not to leave it too often." Faith wrapped her arms around her middle, as if she were protecting herself from something.

Was it from him?

If it was the last thing he did, Beau was determined to prove himself to her.

"I don't mind, honest, Mrs. Thor— Mrs. Landry," Nate said.

"See? It'll be fine, Faith." Beau extended a hand to her.

She didn't move. "I don't know . . ."

Beau held up a finger to Nate, a silent request to wait while Beau crossed over to Faith. "Nate is eager to learn. The office will be in good hands. Hasn't he done well helping you in the past?"

She flicked her eyes to Nate. "I suppose so . . ."

"Do you trust me, then?" Beau took one of her hands. He expected her to wrench it away, but she didn't. Instead, she glanced down at their hands, intertwined.

"Yes," she said hesitantly. "You haven't given me a reason not to."

Beau couldn't help the smile that crossed his face. He'd at least proven himself trustworthy to her. And that was not something he'd take lightly. "Then come with me. Let's enjoy an hour or two away from town."

She looked up at him then, her skepticism finally vanquished. "All right, then. Where are we going?"

"Nowhere in particular," he said as he nodded to Nate. The boy grinned and disappeared into the office the moment Beau took the lines from him.

"A carriage ride to nowhere," Faith mused as he helped her into the buggy.

"Yes," Beau said after he climbed up into the driver's seat. He took off the brake and nudged the horses forward. "Haven't you been on a drive just for the simple fun of the ride?"

Faith smoothed down her dress. It was a pretty light green, very simple, and yet it set off her eyes. "I have," she said, looking down at her lap. "But not for a long time."

Beau was quiet for a moment as they passed through town. "Tell me about him," he said. "Aaron."

When Faith didn't respond, he glanced over at her. "Why do you want to know?" she finally asked.

That was a good question, but it didn't take Beau long to figure why he'd asked it. "Because he was important to you. Which means he must have been a good person."

She smiled wistfully as they drove out of town south along the Stage Coach Road, toward bluffs that arose far off in the distance. "He was. He was probably the best person I've ever known. He was far kinder and more thoughtful than I am. He wasn't perfect, of course. No one is. But he was forever thinking of others' needs above his own. We all came here from Mississippi, Aaron and I, and Ned and Celia. I'd known him my whole life. I'm not sure if I'd told you that."

He shook his head. She hadn't mentioned much at all about her late husband in their letters.

"Well, we came here by wagon," she said, her eyes focused somewhere off in the distance. "We couldn't afford train fare, and besides, we had items we brought with us, household supplies and other things. One of Ned's oxen didn't survive the trip. Aaron gladly left behind a few of his favorite pieces of furniture in order to add some items in Ned and Celia's wagon to ours. It was the only way they could have continued with only one ox to pull the load. And Ned wasn't an easy man to be friendly with, but Aaron loved his brother despite his flaws. That's how he was with everyone."

The way Faith described him, Beau could see why everyone spoke well of Aaron Thornton. And how difficult it was for Faith to grieve his passing. "I wish I could have met him."

Faith scrunched up her eyebrows. "But that would have been impossible. I wouldn't have written to you if Aaron were still alive."

"I know," Beau said with a laugh. "It makes no sense at all, does it?"

To his everlasting surprise, Faith smiled—and then she laughed. "For what it's worth, I'm glad you wrote to me," she said.

"You are?"

"I looked forward to your letters."

"Oh? Was it my cunning wit? Or—how did you put it—my flirtatious manner?"

"You were a perfect gentleman in your letters." She brushed a flyaway piece of hair behind her ear, only to have the breeze toss it about again.

"As opposed to in person?" he said lightly.

"That is not what I meant!"

"I know," he said.

"Then why . . . ? You're teasing me, Beau Landry."

He grinned at her and took her hand. Once again, she let him, and his heart soared. Perhaps she was coming around to him after all.

They rode for some time in a comfortable silence, the horses trotting merrily ahead and the big blue sky above promising a lovely afternoon. All the while, he held her hand and wondered if a moment could be more perfect than this one. The woman he'd fallen for over the course of several letters was real, and here he was, married to her.

"I feel I should apologize to you," Faith said out of nowhere. "For being so abrupt when you first arrived."

"I caught you by surprise," he replied.

"You did, but that was no excuse for me to be so rude." She was quiet again, and just as Beau was about to speak, she said, "Celia told me I should give you a chance."

Beau urged the horses to a stop to give her his full attention. "Oh?"

She pursed her lips together and then looked up at him, her green eyes more clear than he'd ever seen them. "I'm trying."

"That's all I can ask for." He wanted to run a thumb over the back of her hand, or better yet, caress her face as he'd done yesterday. But something in his head warned him not to push her. She was working through grief he could hardly imagine. She would let him know when she was ready.

"Thank you." She gave him a shy smile. That tendril of hair came loose again, and Beau couldn't help himself. He brushed it back into place, but he didn't let his hand linger as he wished he could.

"I do want you to know something," he said. "I'm not trying to replace Aaron. I never could. I'm only me, and I hope that might be enough one day."

She squeezed his hand, and even with the lack of words, he knew she understood.

And that was enough for now.

Chapter Nine

Three weeks had passed since Faith had somehow found herself married again. It was the height of summer, and each day dawned brighter and hotter than the one before. Bees buzzed in the wildflowers that grew near the river while large fluffy white and gray clouds rolled across the sky. Even when the afternoon turned stormy, Faith had never felt so light and cheerful as she did now. At least, not since last September, before Aaron had perished.

She was giving Beau a chance, as Celia had suggested, and day by day, it grew easier. He was a comforting presence, and each morning she awoke eager to see him at the breakfast table or already out in the office, preparing for the day. He kept conversations lighthearted, and Faith laughed regularly with his stories of New Orleans and the characters he'd met there, his life growing up with two sisters, and the foolish scrapes he'd found himself in as a young man. If she'd thought he was clever and witty in his letters, none of his written words held a candle to his ability to tell a story.

Even better, he set her completely at ease, and she found herself sharing stories of her own childhood and even fond memories of her times with Aaron. Josie had visited one afternoon and had remarked on how cheerful Faith appeared. Nosy Mrs. Purcell mentioned at the mercantile—in front of half the town—that married life seemed to agree with Faith.

And it was true. Faith had craved company, and now she had it. But every time her thoughts drifted to whether what she and Beau had was more than friendship, something stopped her. She still couldn't fathom anything else, but she didn't stop him when he held her hand or found a way to stand close to her. Those little moments made her heart speed up—and her guilt kick in.

She was Aaron's wife. How could she be someone else's?

And if she could, what did that say about her love for Aaron?

And so Faith tried hard not to think too much about it. She simply enjoyed Beau's company, laughed at his stories, and was grateful for the help with the mail and the telegraph. That worked just fine until he started buying her gifts.

At first, it was little things. A sweet little carved frog he'd purchased from a boy he'd found whittling one day. A small bouquet of daisies. A simple silver brooch.

But today, it was something much larger. He held a package out to her as he stood there in a new, finely fitted suit. "Do you like it?" he asked, gesturing at the suit. "I hated the one I brought with me, so I had this one made. And I might have picked up something else too." He nodded at the package she now held.

It *was* a nice suit, and Faith let her eyes linger far too long on him in it. By the time she drew her gaze away, she was certain she was blushing again. So she busied herself with opening the package, almost afraid to see what was inside. Whatever it was, it was surely something far more extravagant than he had any reason to buy.

Faith pulled away wrappings until something soft and white and sprigged with delicate green flowers appeared. That something turned out to be a skirt. Underneath, a bodice in a sage green that matched the flowers on the skirt lay in the wrappings, with a matching overskirt attached. Faith drew in a breath. It had been so long since she'd purchased or made anything new to wear. And if she had, it certainly wouldn't have been this fine. "It's . . . I . . ."

"Do you like it? I thought it would look nice with your eyes, and the seamstress agreed. She said it would be easy to adjust if it didn't fit. She took the measurements from some of your existing clothing, which I must admit I pulled from the line one afternoon and brought to her."

Faith swallowed a lump in her throat. He'd paid some exorbitant sum of money for this lovely creation, all for her. "I can't accept it. It's too much."

"Of course you can. It's perfectly acceptable for a husband to buy a new dress for his wife."

She gently held up the skirt, and cascades of fabric fell to the floor. The craftsmanship was exquisite. It was far finer than anything Faith could make with her rudimentary sewing skills. She was only proficient enough to accomplish the most basic of tasks. Celia had always been finer with a needle. She actually enjoyed attending sewing circles and quilting bees while Faith only joined those activities for the conversation.

Beau was right. They *were* married, as odd as it seemed. She could keep this lovely dress and not cause one whit of scandal.

"Thank you," she said, beaming at him. "I've never owned anything like this."

"I'm glad it makes you happy." He took her left hand in his, and then lifted her knuckles to his lips and kissed them.

Faith giggled like a young girl. Whatever had gotten into her, she didn't care at that moment. Giggling felt nice, as did the sweet kiss Beau had left on her hand and the fine fabric against the skin of her other hand.

It was nice to feel happy.

He didn't let go of her hand, instead using it to draw her closer to him. She didn't protest, although some part of her mind told her she should. But his smile was just too warm, his eyes too kind, and his hand too strong. And so she let herself get closer to him than she ever had before. The beautiful skirt crushed between them, but Faith hardly noticed. She was concentrating too hard on how to continue breathing while he looked at her in a way she'd seen him do only briefly before. But this time, he held her gaze, and she thought she might stop breathing entirely and pass out onto the floor.

"Thank you," she said again, simply because she thought she ought to say *something*.

"If someone asked me what I want most in the world, I would tell them it would be to make Faith Landry the happiest woman on Earth," he said, his voice low and every syllable he spoke melting the wall that Faith had built inside herself.

"I feel like I haven't a care," she said softly. "I haven't felt that way in a long time."

He smiled then, his eyes crinkling in the corners. "Then I've succeeded."

"You have." Faith drew in a breath as his eyes searched her face. Something passed between them, and her mind wildly thought he might kiss her now. She wasn't certain what to make of that thought—or what she'd do if he tried. Did she want him to? Would she hate herself if she allowed it?

He moved just a fraction of an inch closer, and Faith caught her breath. But just as quickly as she thought it might happen, he pulled away, leaving her standing there clutching a new skirt to her chest, and looking right at two of her dear friends, Heather, the town's midwife, and Millie, the schoolteacher, who stood just inside the front door.

Faith bustled into action, dropping the skirt back into the box, as Beau quickly moved around the counter. She pretended not to notice as Heather and Millie exchanged knowing glances and—thankfully—didn't say a word about what they'd just seen.

But as Beau searched through the stack of mail for correspondence addressed to the ladies and their new husbands, Faith's mind wandered back to what they'd just shared, and her fingers drifted to her lips.

She would have let him kiss her.

And as wrong as it might be, she was certain she would have enjoyed it too.

Chapter Ten

"Hold it steady," Jack Wendler said as Beau gripped the edge of the wagon with all his might to keep the weight off the newly fixed wheel. "There it is. It's on."

He let go and caught his breath as his new brother-in-law finished up securing the wheel to the axle. Beau didn't know much about fixing wagons, but Jack seemed to know his way around them. All Beau did was follow his directions.

"Did you grow up doing things like this?" he asked as he stretched out the cramps in his hands.

Jack glanced up at him and laughed. "Not at all. I grew up in New York, in the city. The only thing I could fix was a business deal, and I wasn't even very good at that. I excelled at spending other people's money. And making friends—except with Faith, at first. She was rightfully skeptical of me." He ran a hand over the wheel. "Good as new."

Beau glanced about the land where they stood. The farm seemed to be as productive as a factory, at least from Beau's unpracticed eyes. A cozy-looking home stood nearby, along with a barn, several outbuildings, and neat lines of fencing. Chickens squawked from an enclosure, and two horses and a cow

A GROOM FOR FAITH

munched on grass. It seemed Beau wasn't the only one who'd had to learn an entirely new way of life, although seeing all of this made him thankful Faith didn't have a farm. Farming had to be much harder to learn than Morse code and being civil to all manner of people who came to send and collect mail.

"Faith and Celia seem very close," Beau said. "I suppose I'm not surprised she felt protective of her sister."

"She also saw right through me." Jack leaned against the side of the wagon, smiling a little at some memory or another. "I was hiding something, and she knew it."

"Oh?" Beau stiffened a little. He still hadn't told Faith why he'd left home when he did. It was easy to push it from his mind, out here, so far away from those memories—and the guilt—best left undisturbed.

"None of my business ventures back in New York were particularly successful. The last fellow I'd convinced to invest in my ideas wasn't forgiving when the entire venture fell apart. I left town at dawn, but he eventually found where I'd gone and sent some of his men after me."

Beau shoved his hands into his pockets. This was all entirely too familiar. "How did you tell Celia?"

Jack ran a hand through his hair and frowned. "I didn't. She found out on her own, and then I had to crawl out of the hole I'd put myself into. She forgave me, thankfully. And she saved my skin, along with the entire town."

"Hmm." Beau looked away, out across the flat farmland, wheat reaching for the blue sky, toward the large bluff that sat behind the farm. There was a lesson in Jack's tale, one he didn't much care to think about it.

But he needed to.

After accepting a good meal from Celia and thanks from Jack for the help, Beau started back toward town on the horse he'd rented from the livery. Jack's story played through his mind again. The message was clear: he ought to have told his wife what danger he'd left behind in New York.

Beau had left danger behind in New Orleans.

He rubbed a hand across his face. It all felt so distant, as if it had happened in another life. And when he'd left, he'd left more than just the city. He'd put aside the ugly gambling habit he'd developed after selling the newspaper. He'd left the so-called friends he'd made at taverns and brothels. He'd vowed to become the man he'd been when his father was alive.

And he had.

But none of that wiped away the fact that he'd done the worst thing possible before making that decision.

He'd taken a life.

The memory played across his mind, clear as if it had just happened yesterday. LeClere, a man he'd befriended had brought another man to the table that night. A big fellow named Desroches who rarely spoke. But he had a mean eye for cards, and at first, Beau thought the man was simply a good card player. But as the night went on, it dawned on him that the fellow was cheating.

Beau'd had just enough to drink to give him the courage to stand, throw down his cards, and level the accusation across the table. LeClere had tried to smooth things over, but Desroches stood too, irate at the accusation. He tossed the table to the side as Beau began to wish he'd simply folded and gone home, out the money but wiser in the knowledge of who to play. In two steps, he'd pinned Beau against the wall, one large hand

A GROOM FOR FAITH

pressed against his throat and cutting off his air. As Desroches raised a fist, Beau saw the look in the man's eye.

He wasn't going to survive this.

Without thinking and hardly able to breathe, he drew the small pistol that had been his father's, the one he always kept in an inside pocket of his jacket, and he shot.

Desroches fell backward, blood pooling against his shirt and vest.

Beau would never forget that image or the fearful look in the man's eye. He stood there watching until LeClere shook him back to the present, yelling at him to go. Desroches had friends—dangerous friends—and they wouldn't forgive this.

And so Beau left. He made it through a month, when Desroches' friends found LeClere and got Beau's name from him.

He packed hastily and left town that night, hiring a coach to Shreveport and then a train north.

And now he was here, with his guilty secret and men who wouldn't hesitate to kill him if they knew where he was. No one knew his location, save for his mother.

If he told Faith, would she look at him differently? Would she judge him for the poor choices of his past?

He wasn't certain. What he did know was that they couldn't follow him here, and his mother was safe without him around. All was well.

He took a deep breath of the fresh air, expelling the ghosts of New Orleans. The past was the past, and he'd do well to leave it where it was and put his focus on his future—with Faith.

Chapter Eleven

"Thank you for helping Jack," Faith said as she handed Beau a cup of coffee.

The evening had developed a slight, unseasonable chill after a burst of rain had moved through, and so Beau had started a small fire. It was cozy inside the office that also served as their parlor, the coffee was hot with just enough sugar to take the bitter edge away, and, best of all, Beau's warm company with which to while away the evening.

"I don't know that I was much help," he said. "I couldn't believe it when he told me he'd grown up in New York City."

Faith laughed. Jack had been completely out of place when he'd arrived, but he'd thrown himself into farm work, and so far, he and Celia had brought her little farm back to life. And better yet, they were expecting twins. "Did he tell you how much I disliked him when he first arrived?"

"He did," Beau said, but instead of the smile she'd expected to see, he frowned into the fireplace.

"Are you all right?" She set her coffee cup on the little table that sat between the chairs and settee.

He shook off whatever was bothering him and lifted a hand to gather hers. "I'm fine. I had a good laugh over his story about meeting you."

She smiled. "I knew something wasn't right about him, and I was correct. But he's proven to be a good husband to my sister."

Beau went quiet again, staring into the fire.

"Something is on your mind." She leaned forward to catch his eye.

"It's been a long day. That's all." He squeezed her hand and smiled again, but it was hesitant, and it didn't reach his eyes.

Faith had the nagging feeling there was something more that bothered him. She could push and hope he told her, and while that was more in her nature, she opted to go against her inclination and simply enjoy the evening, letting him tell her when he felt the need.

Instead, she decided she would confess something that had been on her mind. "Beau?"

He looked at her, his eyes darker in the firelight.

Faith swallowed. When he looked at her like that, it was hard for her to think straight. "I'm glad you're here."

He raised his eyebrows. "Are you?"

He was teasing her again, and she shook her head at his utter ridiculousness. "I'm trying to give you a compliment. Having you here has been very helpful. I didn't realize how much I missed not having to do all this work on my own." She paused. "And the company hasn't been so terrible either."

"Not so terrible." He laughed. "Your company is not so terrible either, my Faith."

My Faith. The words warmed her from the inside out, more than the fire blazing before them ever could. Was she his Faith? Was that possible? Did she want it to be possible? The thoughts chased each other through her mind until she banished them. She was so tired of debating with herself, with being sad, with questioning every move she made.

Perhaps she would just let it all be as it was. At least for one evening.

And with that, she sunk into the chair, feeling as if she'd just thrown off the weight of so many expectations, so much grief, and so much guilt. Instead, it was just her, this comfortable room, and Beau. It was the feel of his hand wrapped about hers, the cozy warmth, and a feeling of satisfaction.

She reveled in the simplicity of it all. This was how she used to live—until life had complicated everything. Was it possible to feel like this again? Even if not all the time, perhaps sometimes?

Celia's words came back to her. *Aaron wouldn't want you to live the rest of your life alone.* Did that extend to loving another husband?

It was all so complicated, and it felt good to take that thought and put it aside and simply sit in this chair and enjoy the moment.

"Tell me how Celia appeared. Did she look well?" Faith finally asked.

"As well as can be. She asked that you ride out and visit with her."

That was something she could do now that Beau was here. Faith smiled into the firelight. "I will."

A GROOM FOR FAITH 63

Beau regaled her with stories of how inept he'd felt at the farm, and Faith laughed along with him. She told him Celia's stories of Jack's gradual adjustment to farm life—how he hadn't understood that one needed to feed the animals daily or that a man had to rise before the sun in order to have enough time to accomplish the day's chores.

"This talk makes me glad you opted for a life in town," Beau said.

"I enjoyed growing up on a farm, and I would have happily been a farmer's wife, but Aaron loathed the work of plowing and praying for rain and hoping insects didn't destroy the crops. It was all too volatile for him. He didn't know what he might do when we arrived here, but he knew he wanted us to live in town. It just so happened that the man who ran this office had fallen ill and needed to return to Chicago for treatment. He spent one day showing Aaron how to work the machine, and then he was gone." Faith smiled at the memory. They'd been so new to everything—town life, Nebraska, the telegraph. They'd fumbled through it all together, and it had worked out.

Beau watched her with a little smile, and she realized that the memory had made her happy instead of sad.

"We ought to get some rest," he said, standing and pulling her up with him.

It had been such a lovely evening that she almost didn't want it to end. What if tomorrow she woke up feeling the same way she had for months? What if this lighthearted feeling disappeared forever?

"Faith?" Beau lit a lamp nearby and shook out the match. "Are you well?"

"I am." She turned a grateful smile to him. He was the reason behind her ability to simply sit and relax for once. "I enjoyed tonight. Thank you."

He adjusted the lamp and then turned a radiant smile toward her. "Had I known it was so easy to please you, I might have saved some money on that dress."

"I adore that dress, thank you." She swatted at him and he caught her hand.

"I'm glad. I'd do anything to make you happy."

Faith swallowed as he intertwined his fingers with hers and took a step toward her, closing off any distance that had been between them. She was warmer now than when she'd sat before the fire. Part of her wanted to flee—to jump between her bedcovers and hide.

The other part of her wanted to rise up on her tiptoes and press her lips to his.

She looked down at the floor. Where had *that* thought come from? Certainly, she'd wondered before if he would kiss her, but she'd not imagined herself leading that charge.

"Faith." Beau's voice was even lower than usual. His fingers found her chin and gently tilted it upward, until her eyes met his. "I can't tell you how lucky I feel that you chose me to write to."

"I . . ." Words escaped her for one of the few times in her entire life. How could she put two thoughts together in a way that made any sense whatsoever when he held her gaze with those eyes that seemed to see right into her soul, or with the firm but gentle way he held her chin? Faith thought she might melt into a puddle right there on the floor, like wax against the flame.

A GROOM FOR FAITH

His eyes searched her face until she could hardly stand it any longer. If he didn't kiss her right now, she would likely throw herself at him just so she could stop thinking about it.

But she didn't have to resort to such measures because finally, he lowered his head and met her mouth with his. The kiss was gentle but firm. He was holding back, and for that Faith was grateful. She clung to his hand and let every remaining thought flee her mind save for the feel of his lips against her own.

It was all too short and yet it seemed to last forever. Finally, the old feeling of betrayal she'd done so well at pushing away crept in, and Faith pulled away. "I'm sorry," she said, her voice breathy as she looked away.

Beau ran a thumb over her cheek. "Don't be. I told you I'd wait as long as you needed, and I will."

She nodded, a lump rising in her throat at his infinite patience even as her own doubts swirled in her head.

"We ought to get some sleep if we have any hope of being useful tomorrow," he said, dropping his hand from her face.

Faith drew in a breath. "Good night."

"Good night, *cher*," he said.

To Faith's wonder, as she lay in bed a few minutes later, it wasn't guilt or fear that she would forget Aaron that ran through her mind. Instead, she felt at peace. She didn't question why, but instead closed her eyes, reveling in the simple feeling she'd missed for so long.

At long last, her future held hope.

Chapter Twelve

Right on time, Clarence Jones arrived at the post and telegraph office with a sack of mail.

"Afternoon, Landry," he said, heaving the sack onto the counter. "No packages today." The man was still dusty from the road—even his red hair had taken on a brown shade. He took it upon himself to personally deliver the mail after seeing any stage passengers and their belongings from the coach. It always made Beau believe the man saw the mailbag as a passenger itself.

After a quick conversation about the road into Last Chance and one particularly prickly passenger, Jones saw himself out and Beau set to work going through the bag of mail. Faith had gone to visit a friend in town at Beau's urging. He doubted she would stay long; her responsibility toward the post and telegraph office too often outweighed anything else in her life. But he was glad she felt secure enough to leave, even if just for a short while.

He smiled at a letter addressed to Faith. It appeared to be from Mississippi, and she would be happy to hear from her mother. He set that one aside as he continued to flip through the envelopes, gathering those addressed to the same people into smaller stacks to make it easier to hand out when they came asking. He worked quickly, knowing by now that once folks saw the stage pull in, it wouldn't be long before they started arriving to ask after any mail.

Beau added another envelope addressed to the lawyer, Mr. Purcell, to a small stack, and then turned his attention to the last piece of mail.

It was addressed to him.

He immediately recognized Maman's handwriting on the envelope, ever elegant and unhurried with each letter perfectly formed. He sliced open the envelope and began to skim through the letter before folks began arriving for their mail.

She congratulated him on his nuptials and said she would send along a gift for Faith soon. There was news of relatives and neighbors, one of his sisters was expecting another baby, an old widower Beau presumed had long been sweet on Maman continued to pay her visits, and then—

Beau stopped halfway through the paragraph and began to read it again.

I ought to have relayed this information to you sooner, but I saw no need to worry you. However, since I am writing, I thought I should go ahead and apprise you of what happened two days after you left. After an outing that Saturday, I returned to find that someone had forced his way into our home. Nothing appeared disturbed, save for your bedroom. I am sad to say that I found it in a sorry state, with furniture overturned and your drawers emptied. Thankfully, I do not believe a thing was taken. I know not for what the intruders were looking—money, perhaps? Jacques sup-

posed our arrival interrupted them and they scattered before they could search the rest of the house.

Beau pressed his fingers to the paper as his mother's words replayed through his mind. It could be just as she said—a simple intruder forcing his way into a fine home while a widow was out with her new gentleman.

But it was all too odd—only *his* room and nothing of note taken at all.

It had to have been friends of Desroches, searching for . . . what precisely? Evidence of where Beau had gone?

What if they returned?

The door opened, and Mrs. Purcell, the lawyer's wife appeared. Beau slid the letter back into its envelope and pressed it into his pocket as he greeted her. Beau had learned quickly that there was nothing Mrs. Purcell loved more than gossip, but thankfully her latest news about some lady or another was quickly interrupted by Mrs. Darcy the sheriff's wife, Mr. Jarrod whose wife was responsible for all the good food at the diner across the road, and a steady stream of other townsfolk.

With the stack of mail now greatly diminished and no one currently waiting, Beau immediately went to the telegraph machine. He tapped out a short request addressed to his oldest friend in New Orleans, asking him to check on Maman. The telegram sent, he sat back and ran his hands across each side of his head. Why hadn't he prepared for something like this? Why had he assumed they'd give up searching for him once it became clear he'd left town?

What if they hurt Maman?

He stood abruptly and paced across the room to the fireplace. He'd never forgive himself if that happened. Surely they

A GROOM FOR FAITH

wouldn't. Unless they suspected she knew where he'd gone. Although some time had passed since the break-in Maman had mentioned, about six weeks. If they hadn't returned yet, then perhaps they would leave her be. She hadn't mentioned anything else untoward that had happened in the time between that and when she'd written the letter.

The door opened, and Beau turned, smile pasted onto his face and expecting another person come to ask after mail. But it was Faith, returned from her visiting, her face alight with July sunshine and cheer. She smiled at him then, and some of his worry vanished.

"Did you have a good visit?" he asked, stepping forward to take her hat and her reticule.

"I did. Altar was visiting too, with her babies, and it was such a delight to see her. And Millie asked after you. She said you were most helpful to her the other day when she needed to post a letter." Faith looked up at him with that radiant smile of hers, and not for the first time, he considered how fortunate he was.

"I aim to be of service to all who enter this establishment," he said with mock seriousness.

Faith laughed, and the sound of it made it hard to remember what had bothered him so thoroughly before she arrived.

But the worry must have still shown on his face, because she tilted her head and frowned at him. "What's on your mind?"

Beau sighed. The letter crinkled in his pocket as he moved, reminding him of exactly what prickled at the edges of his mind.

"Beau," Faith said, stepping forward and taking his hand.

If he hadn't been so worried about what had been in that letter, he might have been more able to appreciate her sweet, trusting gesture. "It's a letter from my mother," he finally said.

Faith scrunched up her face in concern. "Is she well?"

"She is. She's still seeing a widower gentleman who lives nearby," he said with a little grin. Maman loved his father so much that he thought she might live out the remainder of her days a widow. And yet she'd surprised him. She was, he supposed, a lot like Faith in that way. She'd simply needed time to grieve.

"I'm guessing that you approve of him." Faith tilted her head. "Because that isn't what has you so worried."

He didn't want to scare her, but he didn't want to lie to her either. A portion of the truth would have to do. "Someone forced their way into my mother's house. It does not look as though they took anything. And, thankfully, she wasn't home at the time."

Faith pressed a hand to her mouth. "Is she all right? I know you said she wasn't hurt, but does she feel safe?"

Beau shrugged helplessly. "I don't know." He took out the letter and tapped it against his hand. "I wish . . ."

"There was something you could do?" Faith filled in for him.

"Yes." He crumpled the letter again and pushed it into his pocket, hoping to shove away the worry that came with it. "I telegraphed a friend to look in on her. I hope that between him and her beau, everything will be fine."

"I'm sure it will be," Faith said. She took his hand again and squeezed it. "It's likely someone who will never come back.

Someone who simply took advantage of an opportunity he saw."

Beau looked down at her gloved hand, so soft and comforting. She could be right. It was possible. But he couldn't shrug away the nagging feeling that it was all related to the mess he left behind. Why hadn't he insisted she come with him?

"Why don't I run over and ask Nate if he'll watch the office for a spell and we can eat at the diner?" Faith said. "Most folks have come for their mail already, I assume, and he should be able to handle anyone else who arrives. And besides, he's doing well with the telegraph. Thanks to you." She gave him a dazzling smile that did wonders for the worry that hung about the edges of his mind.

He smiled at her. It amazed him every time how simply looking at her could ease his soul. And ease he certainly needed. As many times as his mother, LeClere, and his other friends had reassured him that he had done the only thing he could possibly have done and remain alive, Beau never could quite shake the horrible guilt he felt from having been responsible for taking another man's life.

Part of him thought he should tell Faith everything, but yet he couldn't stand to see that beautiful face crumpled. He couldn't bear the disdain she might feel for him when she knew. She might forgive him. She might understand. Or she might not, and then where would he be? He would lose her forever. He was almost certain she wouldn't approve of the choices he made that had led to that moment. The gambling, the drinking, the so-called friends he'd thought he had. It was a black stain on his life. And if he could, he would take it all back.

But if he did, would he have met Faith?

It was all too much to think about right now, when her small hand clasped his and she smiled at him. He needed to focus on her, and on the safety of his mother.

"Dinner is a great idea," he said. "Would you allow me to escort you to Dawson's Diner?" He removed his hand from hers and crooked an elbow.

She tilted her head, and placed a finger to her lips as if she were considering his offer. "I suppose I have nothing better to do," she said. "I'll allow you to buy me dinner."

He laughed wholeheartedly, until his belly hurt. And off to fetch Nate and eat dinner they went, and Beau promised himself he would not worry any further until he heard back from his friend.

If further action was required then, he would find a way to handle it.

Chapter Thirteen

A strong breeze blew as Faith arrived at Aaron's final resting place. Well, it wasn't really his final resting place—that was out somewhere on the plains. But this little place by the fence in the church cemetery had a lovely carved cross, and it served as a fine memorial to an even finer man.

Faith stood in front of the cross. A year ago, she never could have imagined any of this—losing Aaron, running the post and telegraph office on her own, a lonely winter with little to eat, and . . . Beau.

Celia was right, she'd decided. Aaron never would have wanted her to live the rest of her life alone, mourning him. She certainly wouldn't have wanted that for him if it had been her who had perished in that blizzard instead. Her reticence to allow Beau into her life had been something else. Grief, of course, but also fear that accepting him would mean Aaron was truly never coming back. Perhaps guilt at having survived when he hadn't. And the sense she was betraying his memory if she had feelings for another man.

Aaron had been so *good*. He always saw the best in people, never held a grudge, and when the town needed men to create a search party for those who had been out hunting when the first blizzard struck, Aaron hadn't hesitated to volunteer himself. His giving nature had been what killed him.

For months after his death, she'd asked God why he'd taken someone so thoughtful, so caring, and so generous. He should have taken her instead. Faith tried to be as kind as Aaron, but if she'd been a man, she never would have volunteered for the search party. She would have pleaded her selfish duty to the telegraph instead. Before his death, folks saw her as friendly and vivacious, but in her heart, Faith was often skeptical of people she didn't know well. While Aaron would offer the town drunk, Otis Ignatius Graham, a warm meal, Faith would secretly wonder why the man simply couldn't put down the bottle and earn his own meals.

She prayed to be a better person, but never more so than after she lost Aaron. Perhaps this was her opportunity. Beau was not Aaron, but he was a good man. And he cared for her. She would always miss Aaron, but if she tried, perhaps she could set aside her guilt at his death and instead work to be more like he'd been. Thoughtful, giving, open. She could be a good wife to Beau if she let herself.

"Faith?"

She turned and saw Josie standing behind her. Faith's friend wore her usual long braid and rumpled men's clothing. She carried a bunch of wildflowers in her hand.

Faith smiled at her. "I thought I'd come visit Aaron for a while."

Josie pulled away half the flowers from her little bundle and handed them to Faith. "For Aaron. I brought these to lay on Vincent's memorial."

Faith took the pretty blue and yellow flowers gratefully and bent to lay them against Aaron's cross. "Thank you," she said, laying her hand on the cross. She wasn't certain whether she was speaking to Josie or to Aaron, but it didn't matter.

Josie took a few steps toward the cross that memorialized her late husband and laid the remainder of the flowers against it.

"It's very thoughtful of you to remember him," Faith said, nodding at Vincent's cross.

"Someone should. As much as I didn't care to be married, he wasn't unkind. And it certainly wasn't his fault he had the misfortune to die in a place where no one much knew him." Josie shoved her hands into the pockets of her trousers as she looked at the cross belonging to the man she'd only known—and been married to—for a couple of weeks. "He was a good person."

They all were, Faith thought. She stood for a time in silence with Josie, each lost in their own thoughts. As much as she hadn't expected, or even wanted, Beau to come here, he'd breathed new life into her. Each morning, she'd gradually found herself looking forward to the day rather than wishing she could go back to the blissful unconsciousness of sleep. She took an extra moment to fix her hair and bothered to add various herbs and seasonings to the food she made, rather than pinning her locks into a chignon without bothering to look in the mirror and cooking merely for sustenance rather than enjoyment.

Beau had given her life again.

She wished she could do something so extraordinary for him in return. Perhaps she couldn't, but she could be more purposeful in her quest to be a better person—starting with him.

And she had just the right idea to help assuage his worry and, she hoped, bring him some happiness.

Chapter Fourteen

The return telegram came later in the morning. Beau's friend agreed to go by Maman's home at least a couple of times each day to help ensure her safety. It assuaged Beau's fears some. The presence of an interested party might help deter whomever was seeking revenge for Desroches' death, and if anything did happen, Beau would receive a telegram.

But the worry lingered. It wasn't as if someone would be there all the time. If Desroches' friends weren't deterred, and if they thought Maman was hiding information about Beau's whereabouts, what would prevent them from hurting her in some way?

The fear lingered there in the back of his mind as he worked with Faith, through the noon meal they shared, and into the afternoon when she left to visit the mercantile. And to make it worse, worry about Maman battled with a guilt at not being truthful with Faith.

She hadn't pressed him, hadn't made him feel as if she suspected there were anything else to what had happened to Maman's home, but that almost made him feel worse. It was as if he'd grown too good at lying.

He refused to be that sort of person.

And so when Faith returned later that afternoon, he decided he would take the chance at telling her more.

"I have something—" she started just as he said, "Faith, I need to—" They looked at each other and laughed.

"You tell me first," Faith said, her faced flushed with her walk home. She unpinned her hat and peeled off her gloves as Beau came around the counter. He gestured at the chairs in their little parlor area.

Faith set her gloves and hat on the small table and sat. Her eyes were the bright green of summer grass, and tendrils of her hair hung about her face. She impatiently brushed a few aside as Beau sat in the chair beside her. He clasped and unclasped his hands, thinking that standing might be easier. But Faith reached over and laid a reassuring hand on his arm, and he stilled.

"I wasn't entirely truthful with you when I received that letter from my mother," he finally said.

Faith's face was impassive. If she was angry or irritated at his confession, she didn't show it. But she kept her hand on his arm, and that gave him strength.

Beau drew in a deep breath. Where should he start? "After my father passed, and I sold his newspaper, I didn't know what to do with myself. I had more money than I ever needed and no purpose to my days. I'm ashamed to say I took up gambling, and not in the manner most men do as an occasional amusement, but as a nightly occurrence." He paused, trying to determine how to move forward in his story.

"If there is anything I've learned over the past year," Faith said, her voice quiet. "It's that we all feel grief differently."

Had it been grief? Beau hadn't thought of it that way, but now that he did, it felt true. Yes, he'd had nothing to do with his days once the newspaper was no longer his, but he'd also missed his father deeply. The world felt less secure without him. He'd been the rock that had tethered their family together for as long as Beau had known. It didn't excuse the choices Beau had made, but he felt he understood *why* he'd made them a little better now.

"I believe you're right," he finally said. "I don't think I've ever acknowledged that I missed my father after his passing." He turned his arm over and clasped Faith's hand. Her touch gave him strength. "I visited all manner of establishments, winning some and losing some. I grew to know men I thought of as friends, and I suppose some of them were, but most were only interested in trying to part me from my money. One night..."

He looked up into Faith's eyes. She trusted him. He didn't know when that had happened, but it was as clear as the summer sky—she'd placed her trust into him. Shame clouded his mind, and he couldn't find the words. How could he tell her he'd taken a man's life? As justified as it might have been, he never would have faced that decision had he not been engaged in all manner of other vices.

"Go on," she said, her voice as soft as the fur on a kitten.

He couldn't. He'd carry his guilt to the grave if only to protect Faith from the worst part of him. "I made some men angry," he finished lamely. "We had a dispute over cards. One fellow had cheated, and I called him out for it. It . . . didn't go well."

Faith gave him a questioning look. "What do you mean?"

"They're the reason I left New Orleans. The man's friends wanted revenge."

"Because you accused him of cheating?" Faith asked. He could see she was puzzling through his words, trying to find a way to make them make sense.

They were true, to an extent. Just not the entire truth. "I fear that's who forced their way into my mother's home."

"What would they have been looking for? Money?"

He nodded, torn between hating himself for not telling her everything and thankful that she wouldn't look upon him as a murderer.

"But they found nothing . . ." She seemed to be saying this more to herself than to him.

"I worry they'll return."

Faith looked up at him. "I had an idea while I was out."

"Oh?"

"Why don't you ask your mother if she'd like to stay here for a while? She'd be safe here, and it would be nice to have her visit."

It was the perfect solution. Beau grinned. "I'd been berating myself for not taking her with me when I left. Although I doubt she would have come anyhow. But now . . ." Now that he was settled and married, she might take him up on the offer. She'd be here, far away from those that might want to use her to get to him back in New Orleans. He'd ask his friend to ensure she left quietly, without drawing notice from anyone who might wish to follow.

"Now is the perfect time for a visit," Faith finished for him.

"It's a wonderful idea. Thank you." He placed a hand on each of her cheeks and kissed her forehead. Her face went scarlet beneath his fingers, and more than anything, he wanted to kiss her properly again. He'd thought about it constantly since that evening by the fire when he'd finally given in to the urge. She looked up at him with nothing but trust and . . . something he hoped might be love.

He may have left New Orleans for the darkest of reasons, but he'd found light here in Last Chance. Somehow, despite all he'd done wrong, God saw fit to give him Faith.

And she was something Beau would never take for granted.

Chapter Fifteen

Josie stormed through the post and telegraph office door and threw the day's bag of mail onto the counter. "He actually paid a visit to George—all the way out to our ranch—to insist I be married as soon as possible! Can you imagine? How dare he. What does *he* know of marriage anyway?"

Faith scurried around the counter, not entirely certain to what Josie was referring, but able to make an educated guess. Her friend stood there, hands on her hips, her face as red as the checked shirt she wore, and hair hanging wildly about her face. She looked as if she'd run here from her family's land, somehow stopping at the stage depot for the mail along the way.

"Do you want to sit? Tell me what happened." Faith held out a hand, but Josie turned and began pacing the width of the room.

"Pastor Collins is what happened. He has some nerve, dictating what ladies may or may not do and how we might live our own lives. I have George! I don't need another man. I never wanted one in the first place!" Josie looked as if she were ready to find the pastor and toss him into the jail for even suggesting she marry again.

"He's moved on from me..." Faith pursed her lips, the realization sinking in. Pastor Collins had made it abundantly clear that all the widowed ladies of Last Chance needed to remarry or return back East. It didn't seem to matter at all to him that not everyone had family there. Josie, for instance, had spent half her life here, outside Last Chance with her brother and parents.

Faith reached out and placed her hands on Josie's arms. She was a slight yet strong thing, fully capable of doing any sort of work the ranch required. "Pay him no mind at all. George isn't insisting, is he?"

Josie shook her head. "I told him I wouldn't marry again, and he seemed to understand."

Faith hoped—for George's sake—that "seemed to" meant "agreed." Josie's father had been a traditionalist, and thought a husband might settle his wild daughter. In the very short time she'd actually been married, Josie hadn't shown a single sign of changing her personality. And that pleased Faith to no end. Josie was perfect the way she was, full of fire and determination. If she didn't want to marry, no one should force her.

"Then you have no need to worry," Faith said in a voice meant to soothe. "George has charge of the ranch and all who live there. Not Pastor Collins. Now, won't you come help me sort the mail? Beau has gone off to help Jack and Celia again, and I've no help for the rest of the afternoon."

As Faith suspected, sorting through the large sack of mail helped Josie find calm. By the time they'd reached the bottom of the bag, she was laughing and speculating on what some of the letters might say.

"This one is for Mr. Travis." Josie squinted at the envelope she held. "The handwriting reminds me of an elderly lady's. Perhaps it's his grandmother. 'My dear Paulie, Please tell me if you received the lace handkerchiefs I sent. I'm certain they will look most pleasing with your favorite plaid shirts. Please do take care not to get them filthy.'"

Faith bent over the counter, tears at her eyes as she laughed at Josie's high-pitched voice. Simply imagining grumpy Mr. Paul Travis, the burly fellow who'd come to town to marry but found himself assisting with various building projects instead, carrying a lace handkerchief was more than Faith could bear.

Josie set Mr. Travis' envelope aside with another he'd received and extracted a bent and dirty letter from the bottom of the bag. "This one is missing an envelope," she said as she shook out the bag.

"Let's see it." Faith held out a hand and Josie passed the wrinkled paper to her. She carefully unfolded the letter just enough to see to whom it might be addressed.

To Beauregard Landry— it began. Faith wrinkled her forehead. That was an awfully cold and impolite way to begin a letter. Without thinking, her eyes drifted to the line beneath the salutation.

We have in our possession one Mrs. Landry, of Coliseum Street. She is well and will remain—

She ought to fold this up and give it to Beau. But Faith's heart pounded and the words made her stomach churn, and it was impossible to stop reading. She unfolded the rest of the letter, which was brief.

She is well and will remain that way provided you give yourself over as soon as you receive this message. Send word to the ad-

dress below that you are coming. You know your crime, and it is past time that you pay for what you did.

An address in New Orleans followed. There was no signature, no name at all on the letter. Her mouth dry, Faith read through it again. A date from approximately seven weeks prior sat at the top. It was just about the time Beau had arrived in Last Chance.

"Faith? What is it? Is the letter to you?" Josie laid a hand on Faith's arm, her brown eyes watching her friend in alarm.

"It's . . . It's nothing. I'll deliver this one personally." She forced her words to sound smooth and unworried, despite the fear that curled up from within.

Josie watched her for a moment. Finally, she said, "I'm happy to deliver these envelopes to the sheriff on my way back to the ranch."

Faith nodded. "Thank you. I know he'll appreciate the kindness."

As Josie took up Sheriff Darcy's correspondence, she glanced at Faith again. "Are you certain all is well?"

"Yes," Faith lied. She needed time to think through this letter. To figure out what it meant. "Thank you for helping me."

Josie smiled. "Thank you for taking my mind off that despicable pastor of ours. Wouldn't it be lovely if another preacher arrived in town and started a new church? I'd be his first member."

"You'd have to get there before every other woman in town," Faith said, a slight grin teasing the corner of her mouth despite the worrisome note.

"Psh. I'm faster than all of them combined." Josie tucked the sheriff's envelopes under her arm. "I'll see you soon."

After Faith let Josie out, she shut the door and leaned heavily against it. She didn't have long before the townsfolk began wandering in for their mail. Only a few minutes, perhaps, to attempt to understand what was in that letter.

Beau's mother was in danger.

The man who'd taken her wanted Beau in exchange. Not his money, it appeared, but him personally.

It was dated almost two months ago, yet Mrs. Landry had written far more recently than that to Beau and had said nothing of it. Had she been told to deliberately exclude that information? Or was she not being held captive any longer?

And the strangest line of all—*You know your crime*. Did they believe Beau had been the one who cheated at cards? That wasn't a crime, at least not one Faith knew of. And why would they want *him*? Wouldn't they prefer the money they'd lost to him?

None of this made a lick of sense. Faith could only pray that Mrs. Landry was unhurt and this letter meant nothing at all.

And that the sneaking suspicion she held that she was missing parts of the truth was entirely unfounded.

Chapter Sixteen

Faith was nowhere to be found inside when Beau arrived home at dusk. He set the wrapped slices of pie Mrs. Wendler had sent back with him on the kitchen table, and that was when he saw the back door propped open. He glanced outside, and there sat Faith, in a chair and looking stoically out across the River Road to the darkening trees and riverbank.

"There you are," he said, pausing outside the door. It was clear she had something on her mind, and he couldn't yet tell if it was something good or something that might make him wish he'd stayed longer at the Wendlers' farm. "Your sister sent some pie back with me."

Faith said nothing. In fact, she didn't even look at him.

Beau drew in a breath. He'd done something to irritate her. He moved forward to one of the posts at the edge of the porch and tried to figure out what it could be. Had he messed up something in the office? Had he forgotten about a stain on his clothing she had to scrub out?

"Faith?" he ventured. He might as well hear what it was and deal with it rather than wondering.

She handed him a wrinkled sheet of paper without speaking. Beau took it and squinted to read the handwriting in the disappearing light. *To Beauregard Landry*.

He skimmed the page quickly, his pulse quickening as he read and his stomach turning uncomfortably. He dropped the page to his side and ran a hand through his hair.

"It arrived without an envelope, else I wouldn't have opened it," Faith said, with little emotion in her voice. "And it's old. Look at the date."

Beau did as she said. This letter was—he did the math in his head—seven weeks old. He tapped the paper against his leg as he stared out over the river. If Desroches' friends had taken Maman, how could she have written to him recently and said nothing about it? He'd already arranged to have her travel here, and she'd responded by telegram. She ought to be on her way now. And his own friend had kept watch over her house when he'd asked. Wouldn't he have noticed if she was missing?

None of this made sense at all. And yet . . . anyone could have responded to those telegrams and he would never know the difference. And someone might have watched over Maman's shoulder as she'd written that letter.

If it was true, and they had her . . .

He pressed a hand to his mouth. He shouldn't have left. No, he should have insisted she come with him when he left. Why hadn't he done that? Here he was now, hundreds of miles away, and unable to find out for certain if she was safe. If she was on her way here, or . . . what? A searing sickness rose up the back of his throat. If anything happened to Maman, it would be his fault.

Why had he been so stupid?

"There is one thing I don't understand," Faith said, her eyes finally on him, but her voice perfectly even. The tone reminded him of when he'd first arrived and she'd spoken to him as if she were locked away inside a shell of her own grief, instantly suspicious of a man paying her attention. "Why would they want you in exchange? Why don't they simply ask for money?"

A life for a life. A shiver chased its way up Beau's spine. He'd killed Desroches. Now his friends wanted to make it even.

"Or perhaps there are two items which confuse me," Faith continued. "Because I also don't understand under what sort of law that cheating at cards can be considered a crime."

It was hard to think, much less to breathe, with her looking at him in that way. Beau pulled at his collar. He should have been entirely truthful with her. He hadn't—he'd been so afraid to lose her—and now it was all on the verge of unraveling.

She watched him for a moment, the growing darkness turning her green eyes into a hazy color. She stood finally, but didn't step closer to him. "When I read this, I had a terrible feeling there was something you hadn't shared with me. And now, judging by your reaction, I'm certain. I can't abide a liar, Beau Landry."

Beau pushed himself away from the post. "You're right," he said, his words resigned. No one else was out here to hear them, save for the river and the night insects. And yet, what he needed to tell her was so terrible, he almost wished he could speak the words into a box, seal it up, and bury it.

Faith clasped her hands together, standing pin straight. "Then, pray tell, what is the truth?"

This was worse than the moment before he shot Desroches, when he thought the man might kill him. It was worse than the aftermath, because despite the policemen telling him it was clear self-defense, a guilt darker and heavier than anything he could have imagined had settled itself into his soul.

"The truth is something I try not to think about, else it will consume me whole. I wanted to tell you, and yet I didn't want you to know. I don't want anyone to know. I don't want to know myself, but that's impossible."

Faith raised her eyebrows as she crossed her arms over her chest. She was growing impatient.

Beau drew in a breath of warm, dry night air, far less heavy than the air that sat in New Orleans this time of year. And he told her the story of the card game, LeClere and Desroches, the accusations of cheating, the way the man came after him and pinned him to the wall, and the revolver in his jacket.

She listened without moving even a fraction of an inch. "He died," she said when he paused.

"Yes." It was almost as if he could see Desroches again, lying upon the floor of that overdressed bawdy house, the blood beginning to seep through his shirt and vest. He squeezed his eyes shut, trying to force the image from his mind. "The police assured me it was self-defense. It was, and yet . . ." He let the words drift off into the air, across the river, and away to parts unknown.

"And yet you chose not to share this information with me. I am supposed to be your wife, but it appears I don't know you at all." Her voice shook just a little, as if the emotion were leaking through the carefully contained words.

"Faith, I'm sorry." He stepped forward then, but she backed away. He stopped, extending his hands and hoping beyond hope she would come to him.

But she remained where she was, arms protecting herself from him.

"I can hardly bear to think on it myself; I feared how you'd see me if you knew."

"That letter." She nodded at the paper that had fallen to the floor of the porch. "I presume it has something to do with all of this?"

He eyed the yellowed sheet on the carefully swept wooden planks. He wanted to grind his heel into it until it disappeared from this world altogether. "Yes. The fellow I . . . Well, he had friends. Men of the sort no one cares to meet. They threatened me before, and I left. I thought that would be the end of it."

"They're the ones who entered your mother's house," Faith said. "And the ones who wrote this letter."

He nodded, wishing more than anything she'd let him come closer to her. If he lost her, he didn't know what he'd do. The fear rose behind all of the worries he had for Maman, even sharper and more urgent.

Faith moved past him, to the open door. She paused, one hand on the doorframe. "For your mother's sake, I hope that letter is untrue."

"Faith," he said as the desperate feeling that if she went inside now, he would lose her forever rose into his throat. It drove him to take a step forward.

She held up a hand, effectively stopping him in place. "Leave me be. Please."

Beau watched helplessly as she slipped inside and out of reach.

*****

Beau couldn't sleep.

His pocketwatch read 4:10 a.m., and Beau doubted he'd slept a single moment. He'd finally given up and spent the last hour alternately pacing the room and sitting and staring into the cold fireplace.

Maman could be in danger.

And he'd likely lost Faith.

Beau sat on the edge of the settee and dropped his head into his hands. Faith had disappeared into her room after she'd come inside, and she hadn't emerged. She hadn't asked him to leave, but that was only a matter of time. He hadn't told her the entire, ugly truth, and now she was not only angry about that, but disgusted by what he'd done.

She'd unwittingly married a murderer.

He pressed his fingers into his scalp. That's what he was, whether he chose to dwell on it or not. It didn't matter whether he'd done it only to save his own life—he'd still ended the life of another man. If he hadn't made such poor choices, he wouldn't have found himself in such a position to make that terrible decision.

But he had, and now he was paying for what he'd done.

Did they have Maman? It was impossible to know. He'd telegraphed the police in New Orleans last evening, only to receive a reply that it appeared no one was home. That meant nothing at all. Maman could be on her way here—or she could be held somewhere else in the city. The only thing it told him was that Desroches' friends hadn't moved into Maman's home. He doubted they had her at the address they'd given him. It would be too easy for him to alert the police to go there. They were somewhere else, hidden away in the city.

A GROOM FOR FAITH

Or perhaps they didn't have her at all. It could be a farce to lure him home.

Could he risk that?

Maman was due here in a few days. He could wait to see if she arrived. But if she didn't, he'd be wasting precious time. And he'd be taking the coward's way out.

He'd run once before. He wouldn't run again.

He stood abruptly, mind made up. He was putting an end to this, one way or another. When he returned, he would try to work things out with Faith. *If* he returned. But one thing was for certain—he refused to live in fear. He would face these men, determine whether or not they had his mother, and then—God willing—he'd come back to Faith.

If she would have him.

He didn't bother packing clothing or food. If he was going, he needed to leave *now*. But he did take a moment write a quick note and to pause outside Faith's door. He placed a hand against the wood. Was she asleep inside? Or was she as awake as he was, tormented by thoughts that she'd made the wrong choice in marrying him?

"I'll prove that I'm worthy of your love," he whispered to the door.

He only hoped he lived to see that happen.

Chapter Seventeen

It was well past sunrise when Faith finally awoke from a disjointed night of sleep. She'd spent hours simply lying in bed and starting at the dark ceiling, attempting to puzzle out her feelings for Beau. And now that she sat up, blinking back the effects of only a few hours of sleep, all of those confused feelings came rushing back.

He'd been too ashamed to tell her. She understood that, and yet she couldn't shake the disappointment and the anger she felt at not knowing the truth. Were there other things he'd kept from her? And how could she trust him again? She'd given over her grief to take a chance on Beau Landry, and he'd failed her.

He was not Aaron. It wasn't fair to compare them at all, but it was hard not to. Aaron had always been honest. Beau . . . had not. And so she'd indulged herself for some time, letting the tears fall. And then she'd put those thoughts away. They were two different men, and Faith was far too sensible to expect them to be one and the same.

One thing was clear, however—she needed to speak with him. She couldn't last night, not when she was so upset. But now, after the passing of a night, she thought she could at least calmly discuss her questions with Beau. And hopefully, he would have answers.

Whether she could accept his answers was something else entirely.

As she dressed, Faith pondered what she wanted to hear from him. What might make this something she could live with, but more importantly, make Beau someone she could trust again? Perhaps, though, it wasn't so much the words as it was the meaning behind them. Would she be able to tell if he was truly sorrowful for not being honest with her?

She wasn't so much angry at *what* he'd done as she was at the fact he'd kept both that and the danger he'd faced in New Orleans from her. It was clear that his actions there haunted him enough. She could tell he felt remorse for both having taken that man's life and for his choices leading up to that moment.

But was he remorseful at having kept the truth from her? Was there more she needed to know? And could he be honest from here on out?

How he approached the answers to those questions would determine whether she could trust him enough to remain married to him. It was a practical solution to a situation fraught with frayed feelings that she would try desperately not to let interfere with her decision.

Because the truth was, she'd fallen in love with Beau Landry, as imperfect as he was.

After twisting her hair into a simple chignon, Faith pulled her door open. All seemed quiet in the office, past the closed door. She made a quick visit to the privy and then stopped in the kitchen. There was no coffee waiting for her on the cookstove, something Beau usually did if he rose before her. Could he still be sleeping? It was awfully late, but if he'd slept as poorly as she had last night, it was entirely possible that he hadn't yet awaken.

Faith considered starting coffee, but thought she ought to check on the office first. Surely Beau would have woken up if any customers had knocked. And the telegraph certainly would have woken him. Or perhaps she wanted to talk to him, to get these thoughts out of her head and see what he had to say.

She left the kitchen and pulled open the door to the office. It was empty.

Faith slipped through the door and stood in front of it, her hands behind her and pressed against the wood. Where could he have gone? The settee looked undisturbed, the blanket folded neatly at one end as it was most mornings. Perhaps he'd gone for a stroll, although it was unlike him to leave the telegraph unmanned in daylight hours while Faith still slept.

Oh, well. Her desire to see this conversation through would simply have to wait. Propping the door open to better hear the telegraph, she returned to the kitchen to make coffee and prepare breakfast. Beau hadn't returned by the time the food was done, so Faith put his plate aside before sitting alone to eat eggs and toasted bread with butter. The first customer appeared just as she returned to the office.

The morning passed in a flurry of customers and telegraph messages. Beau had still not returned, and so Faith pressed upon one of the young boys nearby to deliver the incoming telegraph messages for her. Noon arrived, and that was when Faith began to worry. If Beau had gone off back to Jack and Celia's

A GROOM FOR FAITH

or somewhere else that required so much time, surely he would have left her a note.

She came around the counter and eyed their little parlor area. A square sheet of paper caught her eye from where it must have fallen to the floor beneath the table. Of course she hadn't seen it earlier; she hadn't been looking for it. She swept it up from the floor and turned it over to see Beau's sharp, fine handwriting.

My Dearest Faith,

After our conversation, I realized I have many wrongs to right. The most pressing of which is the safety of my mother. I do not know whether that letter speaks the truth, but I cannot leave it to chance. Therefore, I am riding out this morning. I will board a train in Cheyenne. I promise to telegraph once I reach New Orleans.

I am deeply sorry for the hurt I have caused you. Pray for me.
Yours,
Beau

Faith blinked at the letter, unable to comprehend the full meaning of the words. He left? For New Orleans? To . . .

She sank onto the settee, her hand trembling as she clutched the letter. He went to ensure his mother had left and wasn't in danger. Why didn't he alert the authorities in New Orleans instead?

But deep down, Faith knew why. He felt responsible. If his mother was in the hands of these men, it was his doing. All she could hope was that he involved the police in New Orleans once he arrived, rather than going to find her himself. *If* she were missing, that was. Perhaps he'd arrive and find she'd boarded a train north, just as she'd said in her letter.

She felt sick at the thought of him potentially arriving into danger, but there was nothing she could do. Not from here. Oh, how she wished he'd spoken to her first. She might not have been able to convince him to wait to see if his mother arrived here in a timely fashion, but she could have at least ensured he didn't stride into danger with no one to help once he arrived in Louisiana.

But he didn't confide in her before he'd decided what course of action to take. The page crumpled under Faith's fingers. She didn't know what that meant. Was he so determined in his decision that he wanted to avoid any reasoning from her to convince him otherwise? Or did he feel so guilty for keeping the truth from her that he opted to martyr himself to pay for it?

Her stomach clenched at the very thought of the latter. Surely, he'd have plenty of time on the journey south to come to his senses and approach this in a measured way. Wouldn't he?

She never imagined that her anger at his dishonesty would drive him to do such a thing. Guilt began to creep through her, its long fingers grasping for purchase in an attempt to make her feel as if she shouldn't have confronted him at all.

No.

She stood indignantly, pushing the guilt away. She oughtn't feel badly about insisting upon the truth. Honesty was the foundation of a good marriage, and she had every right to expect it of her husband. If he chose to twist those words into something that made him feel as if he should go thrust himself into danger, that was his own doing.

But the anger soon gave way to fear, again, and as she took down telegrams and helped folks send letters, Faith barely kept a lid on her worry. How would she survive until she heard from him again? If he was so determined to do this, she wished she'd had the opportunity to talk to him, if only to tell him how she truly felt about him.

As dusk fell, she retreated to the back porch again and closed her eyes, wishing and praying and hoping. To have happiness in her grasp and to lose it all over again . . .

It was more than she could bear.

When she opened her eyes, a man stood before her.

A man who was decidedly not Beau.

Chapter Eighteen

Beau estimated he was halfway to Cheyenne when he met a solitary rider coming from that direction. He felt for the pistol tucked into his trousers at his back and retrieved it, holding it flat in front of him while he held the reins in his left hand.

As the man drew closer, Beau squinted into the bright midafternoon light, trying to determine if he was a threat or simply a fellow traveler. As he drew closer, the stranger's bright red hair stood out. Beau knew only one man with hair that color.

He relaxed his stance as he called out a greeting to the stage coach driver. "Jones!"

Clarence Jones raised a hand in response. He drew his horse up alongside Beau's. "I'm headed back to town. Had to get the stage to Cheyenne for one of the other drivers to take over. But Nessa's due to give birth any day now. Couldn't wait to get all the way to Denver and back again."

Beau nodded. Clarence had been the one who had driven the stage Beau had taken into Last Chance. He'd been friendly and just the right amount of talkative. Beau knew all about his soon-to-be-born child.

Clarence scratched his chin. "What are you doing out here?"

"I have urgent business back home in New Orleans," Beau said. "No time to wait for the stage." Beau's horse shuffled, as if he was just as impatient as Beau was to get moving along. He planned to catch the train in Cheyenne that would take him east and then south again to Louisiana.

"You know," Clarence said. "There was a fella I drove in just the other day who comes from your neck of the woods."

Beau's eagerness to move along stuttered to a stop. "What do you mean?"

"The man said he was from New Orleans." Clarence's friendly smile turned to a look of confusion as he saw Beau's reaction.

Beau swallowed as he looked about the plains. Not another soul was in sight. And yet he felt as if one of Desroches' men was watching him right now. "Did he give a name?"

"Not that I can recall," Clarence said. "I take it you don't think he's a friend of yours."

"Just the opposite," Beau said, his attention already turned back toward Last Chance. It could be nothing. It could simply be another man wandering into town looking for a bride.

Or it could be the worst Beau could imagine.

"I've got to get going if I have any hope of getting to town before midnight," Clarence said, shifting his reins.

Beau thanked him and watched as he rode off. Yet he didn't direct his horse toward the south, as he'd intended.

He didn't know if Maman was in trouble. For all he knew she was waiting to board the stage in Denver or Cheyenne. If she was, that meant it was entirely possible that the men who had written that letter were now in Last Chance. Unless it was simply a coincidence.

He looked again toward the south. Something about continuing to ride that direction didn't feel right. Off to the north, he could still see Clarence headed to Last Chance. He'd been so stunned by the man's news that he hadn't thought clearly. He should've asked more questions.

He raced to catch up to stage driver. "Jones!" he called as he rode up behind the stage coach driver.

The man turned around, clearly surprised to see Beau. "Change your mind?"

"The man from New Orleans," Beau said, struggling to catch his breath. "What did he look like?"

Clarence twisted his lips sideways, as if the memory of the traveler's face triggered some kind of involuntary reaction. The reaction made Beau clench the reins hard between his fingers. He prayed he would not hear what he suspected the man was about to say.

"He was an odd looking sort of fellow," Clarence said. "Hair dark as yours, but broader. A big fellow. As if he spent his life laying track for the railroad. But that wasn't the most notable thing about him. He had a scar that went from just below his eye to up into his hair, like so." Clarence demonstrated with a finger. "Had a bald spot where that scar was."

If the reins hadn't been made of leather, they'd have snapped in Beau's grasp.

Clarence raised his eyebrows. "I take it you know him?"

"I wish I didn't." There was no doubt the man was one of Desroches' friends. Beau had seen him on more than one occasion after Desroches had died. Lyon, he thought the man was named. He looked exactly as Clarence had described. Hulking, with hands that looked as if they could crush a tree trunk. And a scar that had taken away some of his hair.

"Did he come alone?" Beau asked.

Clarence shrugged. "Seemed that way. But there were other folks on that stage. He could've been traveling with any of them."

Beau glanced again toward the direction of Cheyenne. The threat against his mother was possible. But the threat against Faith was imminent.

"I'm going back to town," he said.

"Happy to ride with you," Clarence replied.

Beau thanked him but shook his head. "I've got to get back fast. Do me a favor though?"

Clarence nodded.

"Go straight to the sheriff when you arrive," he said. "Tell him I might need some help over at the post and telegraph office. Tell him Mrs. Landry is in danger."

"Well, why didn't you say so?' Clarence asked. "This horse is capable a good gallop. We've been taking it easy since Cheyenne. Let's get on home."

Beau couldn't have been more grateful if the man had sprouted wings and flown back to Last Chance. He thanked him profusely as they drove the horses forward.

It was impossible to talk over the sound of the hoofbeats and the concentration it took to stay on top of the horse. Beau's mind wandered as the miles passed beneath him.

That letter had been dated several weeks prior. Were its claims a farce? Or were some of the men still holding Maman back in New Orleans, waiting for Beau to arrive? Did they grow tired of waiting and send Lyon to speed things along? How did they know where Beau had gone?

They had to have gotten the information from Maman. If Beau hadn't been so determined to keep pushing toward Last Chance, he likely would have gotten sick right there on the road. She wouldn't have given up that information easily. Had they threatened her? His fists clenched again around the reins. If they had hurt his mother, he would see each and every one of them as dead as Desroches.

And then his mind went to Lyon. He had been in town for how many days? Beau thought back. The last mail had arrived the day before, when that letter about Maman had come. So yesterday. Lyon had been there for an entire day. What had he been doing? Biding his time until Beau left?

That made no sense, considering Beau was the one they wanted. Maybe he had to ask about town to find out where Beau was. Or had he been watching them the entire time?

Beau urged the horse to move faster. Clarence kept up with him easily. It was possible that if Lyon had come into the office today and found out that Beau wasn't there, he would have left and waited.

That's what a logical man would have done.

But Lyon did not strike Beau as logical. In fact, the man seemed the opposite of logical.

In his mind's eye, Beau could see Lyon growing angry that Beau was not present. And Faith, of course, would've only had the information Beau had left her in the letter. What would Lyon do then?

Beau's stomach twisted again and he willed the horse to move as fast as possible. The man wouldn't hurt Faith, would he? Not if he wished Beau to come with him peacefully. Of course there was no way for Beau to have known that Lyon had arrived in town, much less had found Faith. But what was he planning? Would he bring her to New Orleans after Beau?

Worst of all, would he take out his anger at Beau on Faith?

A sick sense of fear crawled its way up Beau's spine. There were too many unknowns. Too many possibilities. All he knew was that he needed to get back to town as soon as possible. He needed to see Faith again. He needed to know she was all right.

If he'd been a better man, he would've waited until the morning and spoken with Faith instead of leaving before she arose. As mad as she had been last night, he would have made her listen to him. And, most importantly, he might have had the opportunity to tell her the one thing that had been in his heart.

He loved her.

He didn't know if Faith would ever forgive him for keeping the truth from her, but he knew he would never stop loving her. And Beau needed her to know that.

He prayed hard that he would get the chance to tell her. That he would have the opportunity to promise her that he would forever be honest with her. That he had never imagined a woman as wonderful as she was.

He pressed on, riding hard. He *would* tell her these things, even if he drew his last breath while doing so.

Because if Faith could live a life knowing how much he loved her, that would be enough.

Chapter Nineteen

Faith rose immediately from her seat on the back porch, the man's sudden presence setting her heart to beating faster and her arms to tingling. Not many folks came by the post and telegraph office this late, unless it was an urgent matter. She greeted the man and asked, "Did you need to send a telegram?"

He removed his hat and took a few steps forward, until he was on the steps that led up to the porch. Though the light was fading in the sky, Faith could make out his features when he was but mere steps away from her. And when she did, she forced herself not to react. The man was hardly pleasant looking, with a long scar that ended where hair ought to be behind his right temple, shoulders that looked as if they wouldn't fit through a doorway, and an expression so intimidating that it took all of Faith's will not to back up into the safety of the house.

She swallowed and forced herself to remain where she was, all the while wondering why this stranger had come to her back door instead of to the office around front.

"No, ma'am," he finally said, his voice bearing an accent that was similar to the one that lightly peppered Beau's words.

A GROOM FOR FAITH

"My business here is something other than telegrams or posting letters." He attempted to smile then, and the effect was enough to send up an immediate warning in Faith's mind.

She stood where she was, unwilling to give this man the satisfaction of knowing he'd unsettled her. But her mind was anything but still as it flew through options. There was a pistol behind the counter in the office in the front room. That was too far away to be of use now. It had been part of a set of two, but the other was somewhere out on the plains where Aaron had perished, along with the shotgun. Why hadn't she thought of replacing the shotgun?

Beau had likely taken his own guns with him. There was a good, sharp knife in the kitchen, if it came to that.

Faith prayed it wouldn't.

Leave, she thought. *Go away and let me be.*

"I presume you're Mrs. Landry?" he asked, that accented drawl making her heart ache for Beau. She hadn't let herself dwell on it too much during the day, but she missed him deeply. If only he were here now.

"I am." Her voice was steady, and she tried to concentrate on appearing unflappable, as scared as she truly was.

"I've been wanting to speak with your husband, but I haven't seen him around. Is he inside?" The man's eyes flicked to the door behind Faith.

"What is your business with Mr. Landry?" she asked instead of answering his question. If she told him Beau was inside, he'd want to speak with him. But if she told him he wasn't . . . she didn't know what might happen.

He tried to smile again, but the effect was unnerving. "Well, that's between myself and Landry, no?"

"He's gone to sleep," she said. "You'll have to return tomorrow."

"Wake him, then. This is important. I came clear up here from Louisiana to have a talk with him." The man ascended the remaining steps and leaned one of his massive shoulders against the same post Beau had leaned against the day before.

"I'm afraid that's impossible. You must return tomorrow." Faith stood as tall as she possibly could before beginning to step backward toward the door. If she could slip inside quickly and shut the door, she might have a chance at bolting it before the man could react.

"No, *cher*, that is impossible."

Faith recoiled at his use of the same term of endearment Beau had used for her. It felt ugly coming from this man's lips, as if the word had fallen into the mud and manure that filled the dirt road out front when it rained. She opened her mouth to tell him to leave immediately, but before she could let out a single sound, he'd reached for her arm and clenched it beneath his paw of a hand.

Faith's eyes widened, and the fear exploded in her mind. If she screamed, would anyone hear? The depot next door was empty for the night. The ferryman down at the dock had retired for dinner and bed. There was a warehouse on the opposite side—perhaps someone remained there this evening. Or perhaps someone walked by on the street out front of the office. She opened her mouth, but all that emerged was a squeak before the man clasped his other hand over her mouth and turned her like a side of beef that hung from the hook in the butcher shop down the road.

A GROOM FOR FAITH

He propelled her to the door, saying, "Let's go awaken that husband of yours, shall we?"

Faith pressed against him with all her might, but it was like struggling against a brick wall. The man was a giant compared to her, and all she could do was force her feet to move in the direction he wanted. He pushed her through the open door.

Faith's eyes watered as they entered. Something about going inside felt far too final. He would discover soon enough that Beau wasn't here . . . and then what would happen?

"No loud noises, understand?" he whispered in her ear.

She nodded as best she could with his hand still pressed against her mouth. He didn't need to elaborate on what might happen if she didn't comply; her imagination easily filled in what went unsaid. He removed his hand and she drew in a shuddering breath as he dragged her to the table where she'd left the lamp. He lit it easily before turning his attention back to Faith.

"Where is he?" the man asked, his fingers still digging into her arm.

Faith swallowed hard. It wouldn't take him long to discover Beau wasn't here at all. Which, it seemed now, was for the best. She didn't want to think about what this man might do if Beau *was* here. "He left."

The man narrowed dark eyes that looked even more ominous in the shadows cast by the lamp. "You said he was asleep."

"I certainly wasn't going to tell you I was here alone." It was too late to continue that farce. All she could hope was that she didn't interest him in the least—or that she could reach that pistol in the office.

He grunted, his eyes already searching the room. Without a word, he grabbed hold of the lamp and dragged her down the short hallway. He kicked open the door to the only bedroom, which was, of course, empty. Finding nothing there, he pressed her forward through the door to the office. The room was dark with no fire lit on such a warm night.

He looked about the space before finally setting the lamp down on the table. And then he bellowed into the house, "Landry! It's Lyon, and I've got your woman. Show your face and I'll consider letting her go."

Silence greeted him in return.

"I told you he isn't here," Faith said.

He turned a sharp gaze back to her. "When do you expect him back?"

Faith tried to shrug, as if Beau's leaving and this Lyon's presence didn't bother her in the least. While in reality, her stomach knotted, her palms had gone damp, and she was sure Lyon could hear every beat of her heart. "I don't. He's gone and left me."

He snapped his gaze back to her, that scar shining in the lamplight. "Of his own accord, or did you run him off?"

"I don't see how our marriage has any bearing on your business with Beau." Faith lifted her chin. She'd decided it was best if he didn't think she feared him.

He gave a short laugh and finally let go of her arm. "Sit." He pointed at the settee where Beau usually slept.

Faith settled onto the cushions, forcing herself not to rub her arm where he'd gripped it so tightly. Lyon still stood, looking around the room again. His perusal stopped at the corner, between the settee and the wall.

A GROOM FOR FAITH

Where Beau's carpetbag sat.

In two steps, he'd scooped it up and dropped it on the settee next to Faith. He rifled through what was inside and then looked back at her. "If he's left town, as you say, why didn't he take this bag?"

Faith pressed her lips together. In truth, she didn't know. He'd also left his clothing where it hung in the bedroom. "I suppose he was in too much of a hurry."

Lyon shook his head and tossed the bag back into the corner, where it hit the wall and fell open on its side. "I don't think he's left at all." His eyes gleamed at Faith. "Why don't we wait right here for his return? He'll come dragging his tail between his legs as soon as he loses enough money."

He believed Beau had gone out to play cards. What would he do when it became evident that wasn't the case? "I spoke the truth," Faith said, clasping her hands together in her lap. "He won't be back tonight."

"We'll see. If he doesn't show his face before morning, then you and I will go back to New Orleans. He'll come crawling out once he discovers we have his pretty wife."

Faith pressed her hands to her stomach. She had to do something, but what? Lyon stood with his hands on his hips, pistol easily visible now as the metal glinted in the lamplight. Not that he needed it. After all, what match was she against a man of his size? He could drag her out to the prairie or down to the river right now, and there would be nothing she could do about it. And it was far too late for customers—no one was coming here to save her.

Desperation rose from deep inside, and Faith bit her lip to keep from letting tears spring to her eyes. She was *not* helpless. She had survived so much already—a move from the only home she'd known to this desolate place, the death of her adoring husband, running this office without him as she grieved, being pushed into another marriage . . . and losing her heart to a man she wasn't entirely certain she could trust, much less one she could depend upon seeing again.

If this Lyon thought he could cart her off to Louisiana to use as bait to trap Beau, he didn't know her at all.

He settled himself into one of the chairs across from her, and Faith's mind began to clear itself. Aaron had kept that pistol behind the counter because while he loved and trusted the people in Last Chance, he was also smart enough to know they were living far enough from civilization that this town could draw desperate men. He was resilient and self-sufficient. And so was Faith.

Meanwhile, Beau was the sort of man who could talk himself out of just about any situation. He was charming and friendly, and Faith doubted there was a person in town who didn't like him. What was it that Celia had always called Faith? *Vivacious.* Faith had certainly never felt shy or nervous when it came to speaking with people. In fact, they intrigued her in such a way that she usually wanted to know more about them.

Aaron would find a way to get to that pistol.

Beau would gain Lyon's trust by engaging him in conversation.

And Faith would do both.

"Mr. Lyon," she said with a courage she knew now dwelt somewhere deep inside her. "I must confess your presence here confuses me. Beau received a letter stating that you and your

A GROOM FOR FAITH

friends had taken his mother. If that's true, then why are you here?"

He studied her a moment, as if he was debating what to say. "He never came. So I journeyed here."

That didn't clarify whether Beau's mother was safe or not, but Lyon didn't seem receptive to more of those sorts of questions. So Faith changed tactics.

"How do you know my husband? He's mentioned many friends he had in New Orleans, but I don't recall your name." Faith forced her hands to relax as she spoke. He'd be more likely to converse with her if she set him at ease.

"Landry isn't a friend. In fact, he shot a friend of mine."

Faith nodded, as if she was considering this information. "I'm sorry to hear you lost someone you cared for. That must have been hard."

He narrowed his eyes at her. She smiled in return, trying to lighten the mood. "Thank you," he finally said in a gruff voice.

Lyon retrieved a pocketwatch from his side. As he checked the time, Faith's eyes strayed to the counter. The revolver was located just under where she normally kept the mail sorted. It should still be loaded. After all, it hadn't been touched since before Aaron's passing.

"Are you hungry?" she asked Lyon.

He returned the watch to his pocket and regarded her a moment. Faith kept her expression arranged in a placid, friendly manner. It must have worked, because the harder edges of Lyon's own face seemed to smooth.

"I'm not, but I wouldn't mind a whiskey."

"I don't keep spirits in the house," Faith replied, as kindly as possible.

He shook his head, but Faith thought she saw the trace of a smile. "Women," he said under his breath.

"Oh, are you married?" She tilted her head just so, hoping to convey an eagerness to learn about his family. It was just the sort of thing she'd perfected as a girl, before Aaron had finally made his affections known.

"No," he said with something that sounded like a laugh. Faith smiled in return. She was breaking through his shell, bit by bit. "My mother feels the same way as you," he went on. "About spirits. She claims they possess men's souls and turn them toward evil."

Faith wouldn't have gone quite that far, but she nodded in agreement. "Your mother sounds very smart."

"All my family is," he said, entirely serious. "Maman said the world wouldn't cut my papa a break, else he could have owned half of New Orleans."

Faith nodded sympathetically. He went on, talking about a brother who was so intelligent, he'd been kicked out of school, and sisters far smarter than their husbands. She chimed in here and there, insisting he must be just as blessed as his family. And *that* really set him off to talking about how no one had ever seen that in him, but he was indeed one possessed with a high degree of intelligence.

Faith listened just well enough to keep him talking, but her mind wandered back to that gun behind the counter. He was at ease around her now. All she needed was an excuse to stand and go to the mail or the—

The telegraph sounded, alerting her to an incoming message. Faith didn't know the exact time, but messages didn't often come this late. "Oh!" she exclaimed, interrupting Lyon's soliloquy on the teacher who never believed he could learn sums. "That's the telegraph. It must be urgent, coming in this late. You won't mind if I take down the message, of course?" She held her breath as she waited for his answer.

"Go on." He sat back, seeming entirely at ease with her now.

Faith rose slowly. The last thing she wanted to do was rouse his suspicion. She passed behind the counter, and without pausing, slipped the revolver into her hand and hid it easily in her skirts. She sat at the telegraph as her heart pounded, trying mightily to concentrate on the code that came through the lines. Her hand shook as she wrote out the message, her other hand clutching the pistol on her lap. The telegram turned out not to be urgent after all—instead merely a shipment update for one of the nearby ranches for horses. Someone in Kansas City was working late.

The moment the message ended, Faith laid her pencil down, pulled in her breath, and prayed for bravery. If she managed to escape Mr. Lyon, she'd find a way to get to Beau.

And she would tell him everything that was in her heart.

She raised herself from the chair and glanced behind her. Mr. Lyon was examining his pocketwatch again, paying no attention whatsoever to Faith. Her ruse had worked, and she'd garnered his trust. She bit her lip, wondering what Beau would think of that. She imagined he'd be proud of her efforts.

She drew strength from that thought and wrapped both hands around the grip. Raising the revolver until it was level in front of her, she said, "Mr. Lyon, I believe it's time I see you out."

He glanced up, clearly confused, and then his eyes fell upon the pistol. He hesitated a moment, and then stood, an eerie smile crawling across his face. He opened his mouth.

But before he could say a word, the front door flew open.

Chapter Twenty

Caked in dust and breathless from the ride back to Last Chance, Beau stood in the open doorway, trying to make sense of what he saw before him. And in the half second it took him to register what was happening, he wished he'd taken up Clarence on his offer to accompany him. Instead, he'd sent the man to rouse the sheriff at the far end of town.

"Landry." Lyon's ugly grin fell upon Beau.

Faith's eyes went wide. Beau wished he could go to her now. Take that gun from her hands, ask her for forgiveness, and tell her his true feelings. But that would have to wait.

First, he needed to live through this.

"You're in my home," Beau said in a low voice. How long had Lyon been here? His heart nearly tore open at how frightened Faith must have been.

Although clearly he needn't have worried about her ability to protect herself.

"And for that I must thank you for leaving your letters from Mrs. Landry at your mother's home. I spent some time with your lovely wife. But I no longer need her now that I have you. You're coming back to New Orleans with me to face what you've done," Lyon said.

Beau forced a smile, not about to let this man think he felt anything but irritation at his presence. "It appears Mrs. Landry says otherwise." He nodded at Faith, who still held that pistol he'd seen behind the counter.

Lyon said nothing, but rested a hand on the revolver that sat on his hip, a not-so-subtle threat. Beau could see the entire situation falling apart quickly. Lyon would draw, Beau would pull his own gun in response, and what would Faith do? It couldn't come to that. It would be far too easy for her to get hurt.

"Where is my mother?" Beau asked, remaining where he was by the door.

"That letter was a ruse," Lyon replied. "Designed to get you back where you belonged. It didn't work."

Because it hadn't arrived on time. Thank the postmaster somewhere along the way who dropped it or shoved it into a crevice in a crate or whatever might have happened to delay it for so long. If Beau had received it in a timely manner, he would have hightailed it back home and right into the hands of Lyon and Desroches' other friends.

It was exactly what would have happened now, if Lyon hadn't gotten impatient and come to Last Chance.

Debating the options before him and searching for one that wouldn't lead to violence, Beau opted for trying to reason with the man. "I've already owned up to what I did. I spoke with the police. They agreed I acted in self-defense."

Lyon scowled at him. "I say otherwise. You murdered a good man."

A GROOM FOR FAITH

A good man. If he weren't facing certain danger, Beau would have laughed. Desroches was anything but good. But that fact didn't ease Beau's soul, not when he thought on it too long late at night. "I know what I did. I'm the one who has to live with it. But the law is the law, and I acted to keep from having my own life ended."

"We're not satisfied with the law, my friends and I. Fact is, you're a cheat and a coward. And it's time to pay." Lyon took a step forward.

Beau glanced at Faith. *Don't shoot*, he thought, hoping the words would somehow reach her. There was still an opportunity to end this without bloodshed, and if that was possible, Beau would do anything to keep Faith from feeling the same guilt he did each and every day. She'd already survived so much—too much—to add the taking of a life to that burden.

He stood his ground, silently daring Lyon to come after him. To end this one way or the other. As if the man heard his thoughts, he stepped forward again.

Out of the corner of Beau's eye, Faith shifted, as if she were trying to get a better aim. Beau steeled himself. He didn't know how good of a shot she was—he'd never asked. But he couldn't take the chance she'd miss.

He drew his gaze back to Lyon. The lamplight cast shadows across his face, hiding that long scar that Beau heard he'd received in a brawl that had sent two other men to their graves. Lyon had several inches on Beau, both in height and in width. It was a fight Beau very well might not win, but he'd take that chance over letting Faith shoot.

Without hesitation, he lowered his head and barreled into Lyon. He'd caught the man entirely off guard, and as Faith shrieked from behind the counter, Beau propelled Lyon backward across the floor.

It wasn't enough to knock the man down, though—just enough to send him careening and give Beau a moment to get the upper hand. He drew back and easily landed a fist across Lyon's face. Some part of his mind registered the stinging sensation in his fingers when he pulled his hand back. But he paid it no mind. Lyon had come here, to Beau's home, and endangered everything he held dear. He drew back again, but this time Lyon was ready for him.

The larger man blocked the punch and, quick as a cat, struck Beau in the stomach. Pain seared through his insides as he struggled to take in a breath. He doubled over even as he told himself to stand. He was losing precious seconds to act. Just as he straightened, gasping for air, Lyon's fist crashed into his cheek.

Pain exploded through Beau's head. He stumbled even as he tried to force himself to remain in place. He was no match for Lyon, that much was becoming quickly clear. The man was going to beat him bloody, and if he was still alive, Lyon would haul him back to New Orleans for more.

He still had the pistol at his side, if he was capable of pulling it and firing before Lyon either did the same or knocked him off his feet. And if he was capable of doing that again.

"Beau!" Faith's voice broke through his muddled thoughts, just half a second before Lyon hit him across the face again and a second time in the stomach. Beau's knees buckled, and as much as he tried to fight it, he sunk to his knees. He couldn't go down. That would be the end. He *had* to stand.

A GROOM FOR FAITH

"Had enough?" Lyon said from somewhere that sounded far away. The man didn't even sound out of breath. Beau blinked, trying to clear his vision as he pressed his hands into his stomach. Lyon had stepped back, almost as if he were admiring what he'd done.

Beau needed a moment, just a moment, to force in a breath and drag himself to his feet again. He concentrated with all his might on those goals—just as a shot sounded from inside the room.

Beau's ears rang and he glanced down at himself. Had Lyon had enough and decided to shoot him? But there was no blood, save for what dripped from his nose. He blinked hard and looked up.

Lyon stared at Faith, who stood with the revolver pointed directly at him.

It had been Faith. She'd shot at Lyon—and missed, apparently.

Lyon took a step toward Faith and said something, but Beau didn't hear it. Anger roared inside his ears, deadening all the pain in his body until he stood precariously, his own pistol in his hands.

"Lyon!" he managed to say, his voice garbled.

The man breathed heavily, his massive chest rising and falling as he looked between Faith and Beau who both pointed weapons at him.

"Put your gun on the table and sit," Beau said, trying not to wince at the pain that came with speaking.

Lyon scowled, but he must have known his bulk was no match for this situation—particularly with a woman who clearly wasn't afraid to shoot at him. After a moment's hesitation, he did as Beau said.

As soon as Lyon was seated, Beau looked to Faith. She came quickly to his side, pistol in hand.

"Are you all right?" she asked, her eyes tracing his face.

He nodded. Everything hurt, but he could stand.

"I'll get the sheriff," she said. When he nodded again, she pressed her revolver into his other hand, her fingers lingering for just a moment before she disappeared out the door.

Chapter Twenty-one

Faith had taken only a few steps away from the post and telegraph office when she met Sheriff Darcy, with the stage driver Clarence Jones immediately behind him. She almost collapsed in relief. Beau looked far too injured to prevent any further attack from Mr. Lyon. Faith had prayed the guns would keep the man sitting in that chair and Beau safe, but she'd planned to run as fast as she could all the way down the Stage Coach Road to the Darcys' home just in case.

"Jones came to get me. Folks outside the hotel said they heard gunshots from your place," the sheriff said as he closed the distance between them.

"Yes, I'm so glad you're here. All is well now, but you'll have a guest in your jail tonight." Faith led both him and Mr. Jones inside, where, thankfully, Beau still held Mr. Lyon at gunpoint. "This man forced his way into my home and threatened to kidnap me. He then fought my husband when Beau arrived and tried to make him leave."

"That's the fellow I brought in on the stage yesterday," Mr. Jones said from where he stood by the door.

Sheriff Darcy put Mr. Lyon in handcuffs, as the man sputtered in protest with incoherent words about New Orleans and a friend shot dead. Faith ignored him and went to Beau. She took the guns from him and urged him to sit, which he did, slowly and with his eyes closed.

"I should fetch the doctor," Faith said, settling herself on the settee next to Beau.

He shook his head. "It's nothing serious. I'll be good as new tomorrow."

Faith doubted that last part, given how much pain he appeared to be in now. She looked to Sheriff Darcy. "Sheriff, is it all right if we come to speak with you tomorrow morning?"

The sheriff's eyes went to the state of Beau's face and his dirty, rumpled clothing. "Of course."

"You can't keep me locked up for no reason," Mr. Lyon protested as Sheriff Darcy led him to the door.

"I have reason enough, given the state of Mr. Landry here in his own home. You can tell me your side in the morning too."

Faith bid the sheriff good night and then, after reassuring Mr. Jones that he could come see Beau tomorrow and seeing him off to get home to his wife, she made Beau as comfortable as he could be on the settee. Then she hastened to gather clean rags, water, and bandages. She'd lied when she told Mr. Lyon she had no spirits in the house, because in fact, she had a small bottle of whiskey that was given to Aaron upon the occasion of their wedding. She pried the bottle open now and poured just enough into a small glass for Beau.

She carried it all back to the front room and handed Beau the glass. He shook his head but Faith insisted. "It'll dull the pain. Drink it or I'll fetch the doctor."

A GROOM FOR FAITH

He finally relented, and after she set the empty glass on the table, Faith went to work cleaning the cuts on Beau's face. To his credit, he only flinched once, when she first addressed the largest cut on his cheekbone.

"I imagine I'll look particularly handsome tomorrow," he said.

Faith smiled, glad he felt well enough to make a joke. "The bruising will be especially attractive. I'll have to fight off the remaining widows at the door."

He turned his head then, looking at her, his amber eyes serious. "I can leave tomorrow, if you like. I'll find a judge in Kearney and ask him to annul our marriage."

Faith's heart pinched, and she dropped the hand she still held up with the wet rag into her lap. "I don't wish for that to happen."

His face lightened, despite the bruises rising on his skin. "Are you certain? I understand if you feel otherwise."

Faith regarded him a moment. He was so handsome, even through the beating he'd taken. But it didn't matter so much what he looked like. Especially not after all he'd done for her. "You came back—for me. How did you know?"

He told her of running into Mr. Jones on his way to Cheyenne and how he'd learned that Mr. Lyon was likely a passenger on yesterday's stage. His fear for Faith's imminent safety had overtaken everything else, and so he'd returned to Last Chance. "I never felt so helpless as I did on that horse, racing to get back here. And then when I walked in and saw him . . . And then you, holding up that revolver. I wasn't sure what I wanted to do first—punch him for putting you in danger or kiss you for being brave enough to think of and get that gun."

Faith's cheeks warmed as she folded the damp rag. "I only did what any reasonable woman would do in such a situation."

"No." He rested a hand gently on hers. His knuckles were beginning to bruise too. All Faith wanted to do was cradle his hand between her own and never let him go—but she couldn't let herself do that without reassurance first.

"Beau," she said softly. "If we are to remain married, I must have your promise on one matter."

When she glanced up at him, he was watching her intently. "I know," he said. "I deeply apologize for not being entirely honest with you. It's no excuse, but I feared you would want nothing to do with me if you knew the truth. And while I know I had no other choice at the time, I hated that I'd put myself into such a position. The fact that I took a life will be with me forever."

"Oh, Beau." Faith's heart burst open at his words. She couldn't imagine the thoughts that had plagued him since he'd left New Orleans. "I wish I could take that burden away from you."

"It's all right," he said. "I've come to terms with it, but not a day goes by that I don't ask for forgiveness for what I've done."

As gently as possible, Faith moved closer to him and wrapped her arms about him. He rested his forehead against hers and his hands found her waist.

"I promise never to keep anything from you again. I love you, Faith Landry. I believe I knew that all along, but it wasn't until I was riding like nothing else mattered to get back here that I realized it to be true. I know I'm not as good or as well-respected as your first husband, but I hope you'll give me the chance to be a better man."

Faith pressed her lips together to keep from crying. She pulled back a little so she could see into his eyes. "You are perfect as you are, Beau Landry. And I am proud to be your wife. I don't expect you to be anyone different." She swallowed, trying to find the words for what she wanted to say next. "When I found you'd gone, I was so afraid you'd never return. I admired your bravery for going to ensure your mother's safety, but I . . . I . . ." She bit her lip, unable to put into words the desperation she'd felt that he'd never come back, whether because he'd get himself killed or because he believed he didn't deserve her.

She drew in a deep breath. "I am sorry if I ever made you feel as if you needed to live up to any impossible standard. Aaron was a good man, but even he had faults. And when you left, I . . . well . . . I love you too."

He smiled and then winced in pain. Faith laid a hand gently against an unbruised part of his jaw. He rested his hand on hers and drew her face closer to his. When his lips touched hers, every fear Faith felt vanished. It was as if his love could soothe every pain, every grief, every scare she'd ever felt. Her shoulders relaxed as his other hand found the back of her neck, and she thought she might disappear into him right now and not care one whit if she ever came back.

Beau was everything to her. He was her salvation, her rescue from a grief she never thought she'd feel, and her future. He was joy and teasing and a warm embrace.

He was her husband and she his wife. And together, they could survive anything life put in their way.

Epilogue

Christmas, a few months later...

Snow drifted in lazy flurries outside the window as Faith arranged the Christmas pudding next to slices of pie on a large platter. Behind her, Beau and Jack talked of their growing town with Josie's unexpected new husband and her brother, George, while Josie and Celia soothed Jack and Celia's baby girls in the parlor. The babies had kicked up a fuss not long after they'd finished the meal, and Celia hoped they might nap some so the adults could enjoy the desserts Faith had prepared.

Smiling at the happy chatter and the babies' cries, Faith took a moment and watched the snow fall. After the blizzards, she'd hated the snow. It brought too many terrible memories. And while she'd waited for it in trepidation this winter, she was surprised to discover she found a certain peace with it. Instead of remembering Aaron's loss, she relived how excited he'd been to see snowflakes for the first time several months after they'd arrived in Last Chance. She and Beau had taken a short walk along the river during the first snowfall. With each snowflake, the pain had subsided. And she slowly replaced the sadness with new experiences and thoughts of happier memories. The loss would always be there, but she had so much to live for now.

She placed a hand on her stomach with that thought. It was early yet, and only she and Beau knew about the baby. She turned and caught his eye. He smiled at her, and they shared a moment, just the two of them in a house filled with family and dear friends.

Beau excused himself and came to Faith, taking her hand and leading her outside. The other three men hardly noticed, intent as they were on their conversation that had turned to farming.

Outside, the cold bit at their faces and fingers, and Beau wrapped his arms around Faith. She leaned against him, reveling in his warmth as she looked out across the road to the frozen North Platte.

"Merry Christmas," he said.

"Merry Christmas, my husband." Faith turned slightly, just enough to see him. "Just think, this time next year, we'll have our own little one, like Celia and Jack."

"Pray to God it's only one," Beau said with a chuckle.

Faith grinned. "You never know." She laughed at his anguished expression, and then lifted a hand to smooth his hair. "I'm so happy to have you. This Christmas is a much happier occasion than it was last year." The previous Christmas had been such a somber affair, with few of the ladies interested in celebrating. Even those who had found love again early on had still felt the grief of missing husbands, fathers, sons, and brothers.

Beau took her hand and kissed her fingers. "I agree. Perhaps one year we can entrust the office to Nate and travel to New

Orleans for Christmas. My mother throws the most lavish party to celebrate, and, well . . . I confess I wouldn't mind a warm holiday season again."

Faith nodded. It would be a fun visit, and like Beau, she treasured memories of warm Christmases. "I so enjoyed visiting with your mother. I'd like to see her again." Mrs. Landry had arrived in Last Chance soon after Mr. Lyon's arrest and subsequent departure from the town to spend some time in prison. She'd remained with Faith and Beau for a few months, before declaring how much she missed her gentleman back in New Orleans. They received word recently that the couple was now engaged and planned to be married after the new year.

"I'm certain she would enjoy that too." Beau traced a hand over Faith's cheek, and she couldn't help but smile. She never thought she'd be happy again, and yet here she was. Every once in a while she marveled at the great capacity of love. How much one could love another person, and yet, after grieving that person, still find oneself capable of another great love.

She would never forget Aaron, and yet she knew she was now meant to love and be loved by Beau.

She closed her eyes as he kissed her softly, reveling in the feel of his lips on hers and his hand cupping her cheek. She didn't feel the cold when he kissed her and any worry she might have had flown straight from her head.

He pulled back just slightly and gave her that rakish grin. "We ought to get inside, *cher*, or we might find the desserts gone."

Faith laughed as he led her through the door—into her home where all of her loved ones in Last Chance were gathered.

A GROOM FOR FAITH

As she stood in the doorway and watched the men talk and the ladies stand with the babies, her hand in Beau's, Faith knew all would be well.

Last Chance might be the name of their town, but this speck on the edge of the frontier was really full of new beginnings for all who lived there.

*****

Thank you for reading! I hope you enjoyed Faith and Beau's story. Later this year, I'll be writing Josie's story—I know you can't wait to read about her unconventional courting! If you'd like to read more of The Blizzard Brides series, you can find all of the books listed here: https://www.amazon.com/dp/B08J7D7W23/

Up next is Vivian and Casey's story in *A Groom for Vivian* by Marlene Bierworth. Will the wealthy Vivian and house servant Casey be able to find love in Last Chance?

I want to thank all of my loyal readers—you all mean more to me than you will ever know! If you're new to my books and you enjoyed this one, you might also like my Gilbert Girls series. The first book in that series is *Building Forever*[1].

To be alerted about my new books, sign up here: http://bit.ly/catsnewsletter I give subscribers a free download of *Forbidden Forever*, a Gilbert Girls prequel novella. You'll also get sneak peeks at upcoming books, insights into the writer life, discounts and deals, inspirations, and so much more. I'd love to have *you* join the fun!

Turn the page to see a complete list of my books.

---

1. http://bit.ly/BuildingForeverbook

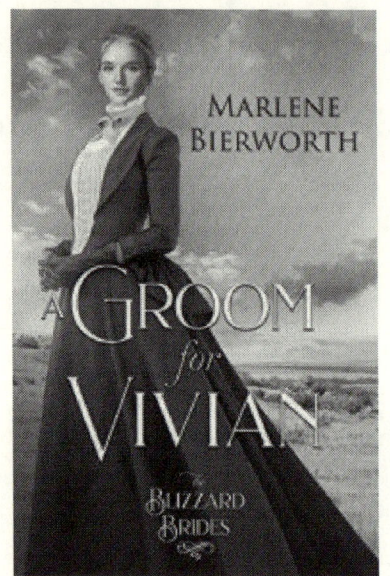

---

2. https://www.amazon.com/dp/B091DF9668/

More Books by Cat Cahill

***Crest Stone Mail-Order Brides* series**
A Hopeful Bride[1]
A Rancher's Bride[2]
***The Gilbert Girls* series**
Building Forever[3]
Running From Forever[4]
Wild Forever[5]
Hidden Forever[6]
Forever Christmas[7]
On the Edge of Forever[8]
The Gilbert Girls Book Collection – Books 1-3[9]
***Brides of Fremont County* series**
Grace[10]
Molly[11]
Ruthann[12]

---

1. https://bit.ly/HopefulBride

2. http://bit.ly/RanchersBride

3. http://bit.ly/BuildingForeverbook

4. http://bit.ly/RunningForeverBook

5. http://bit.ly/WildForeverBook

6. http://bit.ly/HiddenForeverBook

7. http://bit.ly/ForeverChristmasBook

8. http://bit.ly/EdgeofForever

9. http://bit.ly/GilbertGirlsBox

10. http://bit.ly/ConfusedColorado

11. https://bit.ly/DejectedDenver

12. https://bit.ly/brideruthann

Other Sweet Historical Western Romances by Cat

The Proxy Brides series

[A Bride for Isaac](http://bit.ly/BrideforIsaac) [13]

[A Bride for Andrew](https://bit.ly/BrideforAndrew) [14]

[A Bride for Weston](https://bit.ly/BrideforWeston) [15]

The Blizzard Brides series

[A Groom for Celia](http://bit.ly/GroomforCelia) [16]

[A Groom for Faith](http://bit.ly/GroomforFaith) [17]

[A Groom for Josie](https://bit.ly/GroomforJosie) [18]

The Matchmaker's Ball series

[Waltzing with Willa](https://bit.ly/WaltzingwithWilla) [19]

Westward Home and Hearts Mail-Order Brides series

[Rose's Rescue](https://bit.ly/RoseRescue) [20]

Matchmaker's Mix-Up series

[William's Wistful Bride](https://bit.ly/WilliamsWistfulBride) [21]

The Sheriff's Mail-Order Bride

[A Bride for Hawk](https://bit.ly/BrideforHawk) [22]

Keepers of the Light

[The Outlaw's Promise](https://bit.ly/OutlawsPromise) [23]

---

13. http://bit.ly/BrideforIsaac

14. https://bit.ly/BrideforAndrew

15. https://bit.ly/BrideforWeston

16. http://bit.ly/GroomforCelia

17. http://bit.ly/GroomforFaith

18. https://bit.ly/GroomforJosie

19. https://bit.ly/WaltzingwithWilla

20. https://bit.ly/RoseRescue

21. https://bit.ly/WilliamsWistfulBride

22. https://bit.ly/BrideforHawk

23. https://bit.ly/OutlawsPromise

Mail-Order Brides' First Christmas
A Christmas Carol for Catherine[24]

---

24. https://bit.ly/ChristmasCarolCatherine

About the Author, Cat Cahill

A sunset. Snow on the mountains. A roaring river in the spring. A man and a woman who can't fight the love that pulls them together. The danger and uncertainty of life in the Old West. This is what inspires me to write. I hope you find an escape in my books!

I live with my family, two dogs, and a few cats in Kentucky. When I'm not writing, I'm losing myself in a good book, planning my next travel adventure, doing a puzzle, attempting to garden, or wrangling my kids.

Manufactured by Amazon.ca
Bolton, ON